Wonder Dog

I jumped aboard whining and squirming with anticipation.

Wonder Dog

The story of Silverton Bobbie
In his own words

as told to
Susan Stelljes
with illustrations by
Lori L. Webb

fld BOOKS   FOR THE LOVE OF DOG BOOKS
PORTLAND, OREGON

Published by
For the Love of Dog Books
635 NE Buffalo
Portland, Oregon 97211

Library of Congress Control Number: 2004096761

ISBN 0-9761124-7-7

Cover and interior design by Jodi McPhee-Giddings
Cover art and illustrations by Lori L. Webb
Map illustration appearing on page 168 by Paula Giddings

Text set in Fairfield Light
Display set in Luna ITC

FOR
my wandering cowboy,
Buster,
& all my animal friends,
past, present, & future

Preface
& Acknowledgments

I FIRST HEARD OF BOBBIE THE WONDER DOG when I volunteered to organize the archives for the Oregon Humane Society. While searching through numerous boxes, dusty file cabinets, and storage sheds, I discovered an old, framed photograph of a dog. I asked if anyone knew anything about the dog and I was told "Oh, that's Bobbie. He was the original Lassie. His owners lived in Silverton, Oregon, and he became famous for finding his way home from Indiana. He's buried out back in the pet cemetery."

Later, I visited Bobbie's grave. A red and white miniature house, known as "Bobbie's castle," marks the site. His gravestone reads "Bobbie of Silverton; Lost Aug 15, 1923 at Wolcott Ind; Returned to Silverton, Ore Feb 15, 1921; Died April 6, 1927; Owned by Mr. & Mrs. Geo. Brazier."

This strange-but-true tale immediately captivated me. I was determined to learn more about Bobbie.

The trail led me to Silverton, Oregon, where I had the pleasure of meeting Jean and Vades Crockett, the great-granddaughters of the original owners of Bobbie.

Both of them graciously invited me into their homes to view their collections of memorabilia that had been handed down to them. I poured over the numerous scrapbooks filled with letters, photographs, and news clippings detailing his amazing story. I was able to touch Bobbie's original harness and collar. For anyone who has ever done even a little historical research, the thrill of actually handling original documents or artifacts is like a step back in time.

Since then, I have become acquainted with many other Bobbie-o-philes in the Silverton area. Without their enthusiasm, this book may never have happened. I want to thank my illustrator, Lori L. Webb, for sharing her love of Bobbie. Thanks to Vince and Babs Till and Larry Kassell of the Silverton Mural Society for all their advice and support.

I also want to thank members of the Silverton Historical Museum, and especially Jeff Brekas, for additional information about the Silverton area.

Special thanks to Carol Shiveley of the Education Department of the Oregon Humane Society for her love of Bobbie and her support.

I greatly appreciate all the help given to me by the staff of the Oregon Historical Society, especially Susan Seyl and Michelle Kribs, for dealing with my research questions.

I also want to acknowledge the following people for their help and overall Bobbie enthusiasm; Budd Sheesley, Molly O'Brien, Chris Crockett, and the Seiler family of Mount Angel.

I want to thank my editor, David Kelly, for not laughing in my face when I decided to write a book from the perspective of a dog and giving me sound advice on development.

Concerning production, I want to thank Bob Smith of the Book Printers Network and Dennis Stovall of the English Department of Portland State University for their advice and referrals. I am grateful to my designer, Jodi McPhee-Giddings, for bringing her knowledge and talent to this project. She was a godsend.

And, finally, I would like to thank the following people for their friendship while I worked on this book: Lorraine Dee, Jack Eyerly, and Jim.

Prologue

*T*HE STORY I AM ABOUT TO TELL, you might find hard to believe. Some who have heard it say it's all a bunch of baloney. I am here to set the record straight. It's not all baloney, only some of it. Yes, as with all writers, I have taken some dramatic license, but only to protect the innocent people in my life. Heck, I am only canine.

A great many others have tried to tell my story. However, you know how people are; most of them wouldn't know the truth if it bit them on the nose. The purpose of this book is not just to retell the story in the same words so many have told it before, but to tell the story through the words of the one who lived it—me.

I've earned a number of handles in my life including "Bobbie, the Prodigal Dog," "Bobbie, the Wonder Dog," and "Silverton's Bobbie." I've been described as a pioneer, the Lewis and Clark of dogs.

I'm not such an old dog, even in dog years. Yet, I've lived more than the average dog in my six years and I'm not bragging. My memory may not be as good as it used to be, but I remember everything about my trek across the continent as if it was this afternoon's nap in the sun.

1

Wolcott, Indiana

*T*HE MORNING OF AUGUST *15, 1923,* started out just like all the other mornings on our road trip from Oregon to Indiana. I awoke with the rooster, as usual. As I waited on my blanket on the front porch, my ears twitched toward the screen door for any sound of life from within the house. My master, Frank Brazier, was the first to stir. I heard the familiar clip of his footsteps in the hall, and then he appeared with luggage in hand. I sprang to his side and greeted him with my usual moans and groans of complete adoration.

"Good Morning, Bobbie! How's my boy? I see you're ready to go," he said. "It won't be much longer now."

I shadowed him as he stowed the bags into their usual spots on the Overland Redbird. Frank packed every nook and cranny to the gills with all the necessities of cross-country travel. There were extra tires, springs, nuts, and bolts for the bumpy ride over the mountains. There was camping gear, pots and pans, tools, and tarps, as well as block and tackle, tire chains, and boards—for getting the automobile out of sand traps and mud holes.

As was his habit, Frank carefully checked the levels of water, gas, and oil in the canisters secured to the side and front. He tested the ropes to see that all the gear was secure and snug. He finished his inspections and was ready to leave before the sun cleared the horizon, and yet we weren't going anywhere. Come on, come on!

"Guess I better wake up the missus," Frank said as he went back into the house. I slipped in behind him through the screen door.

"Time to get up, Elizabeth. We've got a long ride ahead of us," Frank said poking his head through the bedroom door.

"Oh, for heaven's sake, Frank, why so early? George kept us up so late last night."

"We want to make good time, don't we?"

Elizabeth grumbled something I didn't understand.

I walked to the edge of the bed and nudged her with my nose.

"Bobbie, what are you doing in here? Frank, get him out of here. You know Vivian hates dogs in the house. Go outside, Bobbie," she said.

I snorted indignantly, but I did as I was told.

Later, Frank and Elizabeth came out of the house and headed toward the car. While they said their tearful, drawn-out goodbyes to their friends, I made my mark around the yard. Frank scowled at me just as I was about to mark the sundial in the garden; so I thought better of it.

When the Overland shuddered to life, Frank honked the horn, and I jumped aboard whining and squirming with anticipation. I pawed Frank's shoulders and licked his ear. Let's go! Let's go! As we started to move, I perched in my usual place on top of the blanket in the backseat. My ears and tongue flapped in the breeze as we drove down the dusty streets of Peoria and out of town.

"Looks like it's going to be another scorcher, Elizabeth. The sun is barely up and already it's warm," Frank said wiping his brow.

"It never did cool off last night. I forgot how damp and sticky it is here in the Midwest. Between the humidity and the mosquitoes, I haven't had a good night's sleep in days. Frank, how long do you think it will be before we get to Wolcott?" Elizabeth said as she put on her goggles.

"If you check my black notebook, I've calculated the mileage. At an average speed of about twenty to thirty miles an hour, I figure we should be there by late afternoon," he said.

"Oh, I'm so excited. I can't wait until we get to Bluffton tomorrow to see my sisters. It is a shame that Nova and Leona aren't with us. Who knows when the family will be together again," she said.

Frank smiled and shook his head.

"Now, it was your decision to leave the girls behind," he said.

"I know. I know. We had no other choice. Who else could help run the restaurant? And we couldn't have taken one without the other. Can you imagine the war that would have started over that one? Besides, Leona's the only one who can help cook and Nova's so good with the customers," she said.

"You're right about that. Nova can charm the buttons off a dress shirt. That's why the boys from the mill keep coming back. It isn't just your great pot roast. Nova does have her moody side, though. She must have pouted for days because we brought Bobbie along instead of her. Imagine being jealous of a dog," he said.

"I don't think it was so much that she's jealous. I think she misses him when he's gone. She just loves Bobbie. Those two are like toast and jam," she said.

"She does have a big heart. I'll give her that," he said.

"Well, sometimes I wish she used her brain rather than follow every whim. She's just so impulsive," she said.

"I guess she'll grow out of that. Don't you think that maybe you're just a little hard on her?" he said.

"Well, we all need to learn some discipline. Speaking of which, Frank...dear...I want to remind you about smoking outside when we get to Wolcott. Cora simply hates the smell of cigars in the house. Besides, it wouldn't do you any harm to go without your nightly smoke. Oh, and another thing, please don't disappear after dinner on one of your long walks with Bobbie. I don't want to be the only one stuck at the table listening to Cora's husband go on and on. Goodness, that man has an opinion on everything."

"You can say that again. Don't worry, dear, I'll be my usual charming, attentive self," Frank said patting her hand.

For the first few hours of our ride, I jumped from one side of the car to the next, unable to decide which offered the more exciting view. It didn't matter where we were going as long as we were moving. I loved the ever-changing smells and scenery. We crossed more mountain ranges, rivers, and plains than I can remember between Silverton and here. True, I slept through much of it—except the important parts, like jackrabbits and prairie dogs.

By late afternoon, I woke up from my usual nap just as we reached Wolcott, Indiana. Frank turned down a side street and coasted the Overland to a stop in front of a large, yellow house. As Frank and Elizabeth got out of the auto, several people came from the house to greet them. I jumped off from my roost in the back and began to explore. A gray-haired woman, about the same age as Elizabeth, called out in a high-pitched voice that hurt my ears.

"Elizabeth, oh, Elizabeth, you made it. You're finally here! All the way from Oregon! It's so good to see you," she said.

"Cora, you haven't changed a bit. How do you stay so slim? I am just green with envy," Elizabeth squealed back.

There were overlapping shouts of joy, hugs, and kisses, and a flurry of bags unloaded. The women fluttered around Elizabeth like so many bees around honeysuckle and escorted her into the house. The smell of lavender wafted in their wake.

As Frank toted the suitcases behind, a short, balding man who smelled of boot polish helped him.

"How was your trip, Frank? Did you have any trouble crossing the Rockies? I hope you took the Lincoln Highway like I recommended," the bald man said.

"Yes, I did just as you suggested, Joe. First, we took Oregon Trail Highway through Idaho. And then, in Granger, Wyoming, I got onto the Lincoln which took us through the South Pass and over the Divide between Laramie and Cheyenne. It's amazing! The highway is brick and pavement nearly all the way across now. Or at least good-graded gravel. There are a few stretches of dirt roads, but they're well maintained for the most part. The new Overland held up fine. We had a few flat tires outside of Point of Rocks, Wyoming, but that's to be expected. They don't call it Point of Rocks for nothing! Ha! Let's see, the speedometer reads 2,550 miles. Not bad, huh!" he said.

"Well, it's a fine-looking machine. That's some color you picked out," Joe said.

"Nova calls it apple red," Frank said.

"No, Frank. Candy-apple red. She says the color reminds her of the candy apples in Cunningham's Confectionary," Elizabeth said.

"That's right. Candy-apple red. Of course, she is a bit dusty from the road. But she sure does shine like an apple after a good wax," Frank said.

"I must say I thought Frank had gone a little strange in the head when he picked such a flashy car. However, I've become used to all the attention. You see all colors of automobiles on the roads these days," she said.

"She drives like a dream. Easy to maneuver. Light as a cloud. Good springs. Remember when we drove to Oregon the first time, Elizabeth? I swear that old jalopy was always breaking down. This time, for the most part, it was smooth sailing all the way. Why, I bet there were times, especially across Nebraska, that the Overland reached forty five miles an hour," Frank said.

"And I had to remind him, more than once, that the speed limit was only fifteen miles an hour," Elizabeth said.

"Well, when you're on the wide open road, you forget about speed limits," Frank said as he placed the suitcases by the front door.

"Elizabeth, I'm taking the car into a service station in town before everything closes up. Hey, Joe, my carburetor needs adjusting, do you know of a mechanic's shop I can go to?"

"There's a place on the east end of town. On Oak Street. Just head in that direction. Oak is one street over to your right. You might want to get there pretty soon. I think they close up around five," Joe said.

"I better get a move on then. I'll meet you back here in a little while, Elizabeth. See you folks later," Frank said.

I was busy making my mark on Cora's hydrangeas, when Frank called out to me.

"You want to come, Bobbie?" he said.

Yes, oh, yes, I wag. Anything is better than confinement to the front porch with nothing to do. I jumped onto the back rack above the spare tire as the Overland chugged to life again. This was my favorite spot for short jaunts about town. It allowed me the freedom to jump off and chase things every now and then.

Accompanying Frank as he tended to the Overland's many needs was something I was used to. We had visited every mechanic's shop, way station, garage, blacksmith's, gas pump, water pump, rest stop, campground, and tourist camp between Oregon and Indiana.

Soon, Frank pulled into a run down mechanic's shop on the edge of a scrap yard. From the minute we pulled in, I didn't like the smell of the joint and my hackles were up. Rusty truck carcasses and puddles of oil littered the yard. The ramshackle garage looked as if a good sneeze would topple it.

The owner, Chester, was a large, odorous man who waddled and wheezed as he moved about the shop. Grease stains covered his overalls from chin to toe, and his fingers were so black you couldn't tell where his hands began and the dirty cuffs left off. The entire time he talked with Frank, he clenched the wet stub of a cigar between large, yellow teeth.

While Frank and Chester discussed the carburetor, I jumped out of the car to stretch my legs. I spotted a large, orange cat with paws the size of catcher's mitts. He looked like he was good for some short-term amusement.

I was sniffing about—minding my own business, marking a pile of old tires—when a bulldog, the size of a small tractor, came out of nowhere and charged toward me. Normally, I can hold my own against any dog, and I was prepared to do so at this point. I had encountered his sort before, a real rube who found it necessary to push his weight around to feel superior. His large head had nothing to do with his brain.

Flecks of foam and drool spewed from his mouth. His curled lips exposed long razor-sharp teeth. I approached him in a friendly but cautious manner with my head up, ears cocked, and tail at half-mast.

With his hackles up, he walked stiffly toward me. He stared directly at me with his head lowered down, growling from the back of his throat. I knew he meant business, but I wasn't going to back down. I faced him, eyeball to eyeball. When I refused to look away, he tore into me. In an instant, I was on my back with the bulldog's huge jaws around my throat. With my rear legs, I thrust him off me and he tumbled backward. He lunged for me again. I dodged to the side and took a slice out of his ear before he turned to face me again. He shook his head in surprise, and blood splattered in all directions. Now he was really mad. He ran toward me at full speed using his powerful chest like a battering ram. I would have held my own against him, but the sound of his snarling brought a number of his ilk from around the side of the building. I knew I didn't have a chance against such a pack of bloodthirsty cut-throats. So, with the bulldog steadily breathing down my neck, I did what I have never done before—I ran. I ran as if my life depended on it.

Frank called out to me, "Bobbie, Bobbie, come back," as I ran down the alley and around the corner. But I didn't stop. I sped down strange streets, past a blur of buildings. My only instinct was to get as far away as possible.

I ran until the air burned in my lungs, and my legs felt like stones. Finally, in front of a produce market, I turned to fight them with my last breath. A grocer, who was sweeping debris into the gutter, swung his broom at the mangy group of pikers.

"Get outta here you mongrels. I'm sick and tired of you running around my shop and scaring off my customers. Scram!" he bellowed. He swung wildly and scattered them in all directions as I made my escape.

I slipped into a stairwell where I laid low until I could catch my breath. Later, when it was all clear, I crawled out and searched for Frank. I looked all around me in a panic. I couldn't remember the way I had come. I had run down so many streets and alleyways, but I didn't pay attention to anything. Nothing looked familiar. It was all so strange and confusing. I was completely lost.

I didn't know what to do. I wandered for hours, searching all the faces of the people on the street in hopes that they could be Frank or Elizabeth. I couldn't find them or a trace of their scent. I never felt so afraid and alone.

I wandered the strange streets until past dark, when suddenly I detected the oily smell of the mechanic's shop, and the smell of his greasy dog. I eventually found the shop, which was now as quiet as a church the day after Christmas.

The sleeping hulk of the bulldog spilled out of his ramshackle doghouse. By his grunts, snorts, and twitches, I could tell he was relishing in a phantom pursuit. I approached cautiously, as I didn't want to wake him and have a repeat of the afternoon's events.

I looked around, but I didn't see Frank or the Overland. My heart

...a bulldog, the size of a small tractor, came out of nowhere...

sank. Would I ever be able to find them? Were they looking for me? If only I could remember the way back to the house where we had first stopped. The trouble with being a passenger is that you don't really pay attention to where you are going. I had slept most of the way across Nebraska.

I didn't know what to do. I was tired, so I decided to stay put for the night. I crawled behind some old boxes up against the building and tried to get some rest.

However, I found it difficult to sleep. What would my family do without me? It was my job to look after them, to keep them in a group. Without me, they were likely to wander off. How I missed them. I was no longer curious, just hungry, tired, and a little lonely. I lay in that dark, smelly place, drifting in and out of sleep. My stomach wouldn't stop grumbling. I thought about the warm meat that Elizabeth would have ready for me. *Too tired to look for food. The leftovers of the bulldog's dinner smell good. Don't trust that chain around his neck. Better not tempt…*

I fell asleep and dreamt about my early days on the Seiler farm in Mount Angel, Oregon, when I first learned about cows.

2

Dog in the Manger

MY BROTHER AND I were huddled next to our dad, Gypsy, as he was telling us a story.

"The two of you were born sometime in February of this year, *1921*. I don't remember the exact date, and your mother did not keep records. I remember it was a dark and stormy night, and the day was not much better. It rained cats and dogs, and then Great Danes. All day and night, the wind rattled the house. I was wound up like a terrier chasing his tail. I drove your mother crazy. Her mood was as black as my nose. Every time I came near her, she shot me a look as if I was to blame for the storm, too. So I just cleared out of the way," he said.

Our mother, Lady, didn't have much to say about the day we were born, except to say how much suffering she went through to bring us into the world. Mother was not the complaining type, but she rolled her eyes and sighed.

"It took all night and into the morning before I was able to rest. After you were born, your other brothers and sisters never moved, even after I gave them a thorough licking. Another simply went to sleep and never woke up again. I've seen it happen before to other mothers, but you don't really know how it feels until it happens to you," she said.

She fell silent for a moment, leaned her head down, and gave me a soft lick across my backside.

"That is why the two of you are even more precious," she said.

Before my eyes opened, my earliest memory was of nuzzling with my mother in a hay-filled, wooden box in the barn. I loved the smell and warmth of her. Most of the time, I slept or wriggled over the top of my littermate in search of a nipple. Mother would nudge us with her nose or lick our backsides despite our greediness.

After my eyes opened, I grabbed every opportunity to get out of the wooden box and explore the farm. From early on, I was fascinated with anything that moved: cats, kittens, frogs, gophers, but I was especially entranced with poultry. The mere sight of a mother hen with her brood of chicks would send me flying across the barnyard. I loved to chase the little fluff balls as they scurried about. I meant no harm. I just liked keeping them in groups.

The mother hen clucked indignantly, ruffled her feathers, and attacked me with her sharp beak. But this didn't stop me. However, when Mrs. Seiler complained about the drop in egg production, they put a stop to my daily round-up.

I then turned my attention to the ducks on the pond. They proved to be more difficult to keep in groups, as they could glide across the water and disappear into the reeds. I was not nearly as swift in the water as I was on land, so they had the advantage.

I discovered that all my efforts herding chicks, ducks, and kittens did not go to waste.

Soon, I was shadowing my parents as they worked about the farm. It was their job to herd the cows to and from the barn each day for the milking.

One morning, they were in the pasture even before Mr. Seiler had his shoes on. Mother ran to the far side of the pasture circling the herd. Her long, copper coat and white ruff glistened in the morning sun. She was a real beaut, if I do say so myself.

At one point, a tawny calf scampered away from the group. Mother was off in a flash. Coming round in front of the straggler, she crouched close to the ground, froze, and locked her golden eyes upon him. The calf stood still for a few moments with a confused look on its face, his wide eyes staring back. Then he turned uneasily and joined the rest of the herd.

As soon as the frisky calf was in line, an older, black-faced cow stopped in her tracks and refused to budge. With his arm outstretched,

Mr. Seiler whistled and signaled to my dad to go to the rear of the herd.

"Come-bye, Gypsy, get Duchess," he said.

Dad made a half circle around the rear of the herd and came up behind, barking furiously at Duchess, who remained rooted to a clump of grass by the fence. She refused to budge, so I joined in the fray by yapping and circling Duchess just as Dad was doing.

The discontented cow bellowed as she turned to face me, her eyes bulging out their sockets. Dad moved around to her front again. Barking even more furiously, he moved in closer and gave her a good nip in the nose. Duchess took off like an indignant, fat rabbit, her legs kicking blindly behind her.

"Gypsy, get back! DOWN!" Mr. Seiler yelled. "What do you think you are doing? You know better than that! A fine example you are setting for your sons."

Dad stopped dead in his tracks and lay down, his ears pasted back against his head.

I raced after Duchess trying to give her a nip just as I had seen Dad do. Mother appeared out of nowhere and came between the cow and me. With her mouth, she scruffed me by the back of the neck and carried me out of hooves way.

When we were clear of the herd, she plopped me down, placed her jaw around my muzzle, and glared at me.

I was mortified. Mother had never scolded me before. The only thing I could manage was to puddle beneath me. That was the last day I took a cow on with my teeth.

3

Going in Circles

I AWOKE TO THE MOURNFUL WHISTLE of a distant train. At first, I didn't remember where I was, but then it sank in. I was lost. I needed to find my family. I left the mechanic's shop before the sun came up and searched for hours for some sign of them or the Overland.

I often circled back to the mechanic's shop since that was the last place I had seen Frank. Chester spotted me once and called out as his dog lunged at his chain, but I kept my distance.

However, I did detect traces of both Frank and Elizabeth's scent, which told me that they had been there recently.

I followed their scent trail out of town into unfamiliar territory. I traveled for days not knowing what direction I was heading. There was still no sign of them, and the scent trail became as cold as a discarded hot dog on a sidewalk in January.

I searched for food wherever I could: behind restaurants and butcher shops, at tourist camps, and where road crews ate lunch. I dodged brooms and old vegetables more times that I can remember. Other dogs relentlessly hounded and chased me, even before I could make my mark.

Every town I came to I searched the tourist camps and mechanic shops in hope that Frank and Elizabeth or the Overland were there.

I traveled for days not knowing what direction I was heading.

At one camp, I detected Frank and Elizabeth's faint scent mixed in with those of other travelers, but I did not find them. I felt as if I was going in circles. I was tired and hungry all the time, but I kept looking.

After traveling for several days, I came to another small town among many others that I had passed through. I stuck to the alleyways to stay out of the way of shopkeepers with brooms or the bulls in blue uniforms. I was searching for some food when I detected some nice, ripe garbage cans. I approached cautiously. The way seemed clear. The cans had been overturned, and there were scraps of food strewn across the ground. I detected the musky odor of raccoons, maybe possum. I was in luck. I gorged on soggy bread and old potatoes. I found a bone with some fatty meat still attached. People throw away the best part of the cow. I was sneaking off, when I heard a voice behind me.

"So, what do you think you're up to?" the voice asked. I spun around and saw a young man watching me. He smiled as he swept the hair away from his eyes. He knelt down and held his hand out to me.

"It's all right boy, come here. Are you hungry?" he said. I stood with the bone hanging from my mouth, ready to flee at a moment's notice.

"It's OK boy, come here. I won't hurt you. There's a good boy."

I relaxed and walked slowly toward him. He held out his hand to me, but I stopped short of his reach. He smiled and waited patiently. We eyed each other for a few moments, but I kept my distance.

"Stay here boy," he said as he got up and went inside the house. Shortly after, he returned with a pan full of food scraps. He set it down on the ground and stepped back a few feet.

I put the bone down and straddled the plate. I ate the scraps in about three large gulps and a couple of good swipes of the tongue. I wouldn't have minded if there was more of the same.

The man sat down on the worn, wooden steps leading from his back door and kept talking.

"You poor thing! You were hungry weren't you? Where did you come from boy? I see you have a collar on. You must belong to somebody. I've never seen you around here before. I wonder where your owners are. They must be frantic wondering about you. You look well cared for. You're a very nice-looking dog. Yes you are."

He wasn't such a bad sort. I gave him a flick of the tail.

"Have you had enough to eat?" he asked. I gave him a sharp bark. Never enough!

He got up and walked toward me. I grabbed my bone, stepped back a few feet, and was ready to run. He simply picked up the empty pan and held his hand out to me. I gave him a good sniff. He reached under and scratched my chin.

He then went back onto the porch, sat in a chair, and put his feet up on the porch railing. I watched him and he watched me.

I lay down on the grass at the bottom of the steps next to my bone. After awhile, my eyelids became heavy, and I closed my eyes. As I drifted in and out of sleep, I dreamt of a day almost two years ago when I met some other strangers.

4

Love at First Sight

I WAS STILL A PUP living with Mom and Dad on the Seiler farm. No longer a whelp, but still with an awkwardness that could be embarrassing.

One day, an automobile pulled up the long drive and stopped outside our farmhouse. A middle-aged man and woman stepped out, along with two younger women. They walked toward the fenced yard where I was playing with my brother.

As the man approached, he took off his felt hat and introduced himself to Mr. Seiler.

"Good day! I'm Frank Brazier. This is my wife, Elizabeth, and my stepdaughters, Nova and Leona. We saw the sign by the road that you have collie pups for sale. We came to take a look," he said.

"How do you do? Carl Seiler," my master said shaking hands with Frank.

"My family and I work a farm over by Silverton. We sure could use a good dog to help with our milk cows," Frank said.

"Well, you've come to the right place. We have two good pups. Come and take a look," Mr. Seiler said pointing in our direction.

Nova leaned over the fence to get a better look. Her dark eyes sparkled as she gave us a big grin. A mop of short, wavy brown hair bounced around her bright face. She was a real beaut.

"Oh, they're both so cute, how can we ever pick just one?" she said.

I tumbled with my brother, but kept one eye on the newcomers. When I chomped down on his muzzle, he yelped and ran off. I crouched and lunged. Chewed and growled. When Nova laughed, I knew I had her attention.

"Look at the one with the bobtail. Isn't he just the most full-of-life pup you ever saw? He's not even the biggest, and yet he acts as if he is. He's so cute. Please, Mr. Seiler, can I get in with them to visit?" she said.

Mr. Seiler laughed and said, "Go right ahead. Take all the time that you need."

Nova quickly came through the gate and ran toward us.

At first, Mother tried to block her way, but Nova stroked her head and chest.

"What's the mama's name, Mr. Seiler?" she said.

"Her name is Lady. She's a pure-bred Scotch collie. That's Gypsy, the father. He's Scotch collie and English shepherd mix. Don't hold his background against him. He's a good herder. They're both good herding dogs. I would rather lose my right arm than lose Gypsy or Lady," Mr. Seiler said.

"Lady's beautiful. Look at her white chest. She certainly is a lady," Nova said as she stroked my mother.

If anything could sway my mother, it was flattery. Vanity was her only weakness. She let Nova get by to look at us.

"Come here puppies. Come on," she said clapping her hands. We ran toward her, grabbing for her hemline and shoelaces. I went for the socks. She plopped down on the ground laughing as we licked and nipped at her hands and chin. Eventually, my brother lost interest, and I was alone with Nova.

She petted me all over with light, delicate fingers, and cradled me next to her shoulder. Then she got up, and ran about slowly while I chased her barking and nipping at her heels.

"Ouch! Gosh his little teeth are sharp," she said rubbing her ankles.

"Well, Nova, if you didn't get him all riled up he wouldn't bite," Leona said.

"He's just playing. That's the way puppies are. They'll bite anything," Nova said as she ran around.

At this point, Frank came through the gate and gave out a little whistle. I perked up my ears and ran toward him. He bent down to my level as I came up to him.

I chewed his thumb, but he took it away and firmly said "No." I really didn't have a firm concept of "no" at that time, so he had to work with me for a while. At any rate, I must have pleased him, for he smiled and patted me on the head.

He walked slowly around the pen, whistling and patting his leg as I followed. Sometimes, the cuff of his pants distracted me, or I would run back to Nova, but Frank whistled again or called "Come here, boy" and I trotted back to him. He gave me a big smile, patted me on the head, and said "Good Boy."

"He listens well. He may be a bit headstrong, but not without some sense," Frank said. "What do you think, Elizabeth?"

Elizabeth was laughing so hard the jowls around her neck jiggled.

"Well, he's not the best looking one or the biggest, but he sure has a lot of spunk. A bit of a clown as well. Those lop-sided ears give him a devil-may-care look about him," she said wiping her tears from beneath her glasses.

"To me he has a look like 'Here comes trouble!'" Leona said.

"He takes after his father in the looks department. His coat is darker like Gypsy's as well," Mr. Seiler said.

"He does seem to have the right temperament for working cows. He's sharp. He knows what is going on around him," Frank said.

"I don't even have to think about it, this is the one I want," Nova said as she scooped me up.

Leona shook her head and pursed her lips.

"I don't know. Don't you think he's just a bit wild? We need a dog we can rely on, and one who obeys. That one looks like he has a mind of his own, much like you, Nova. No wonder you like him."

Nova tossed her head.

"I don't care. I vote for this one. There is nothing wrong with a dog that has some spirit. I bet he would liven things up around the farm," she said as she bounced me in her arms while I chewed on her ear.

"Now, Leona, you have a point about needing a dog we can rely on, but I think this pup's pretty attentive. He came when called. Did you see the way he followed me? You can see he is a born herder. I can break him of that nipping habit in time. All pups bite…but it doesn't help to encourage them," Frank said winking at Nova.

Frank and Elizabeth examined my ears and mouth. After a thorough inspection, and despite Leona's misgivings, they decided I would do.

Nova picked me up and held me close. I liked this sweet-smelling young girl.

"Look at his little tail go! He sure is a happy fellow. I know. Let's call him Bobbie, for his bobtail," Nova said.

"Isn't that a rather ordinary, predictable name? Can't we choose something more dignified, like Prince or Lad?" Leona said.

"He just seems like a Bobbie to me. Bobbie. That's the name of a scamp. I feel this guy is a real scamp. Aren't you Bobbie? Bobbie. My little bobbin," Nova said as she gently tugged at my ears.

"He does look more like a Bobbie than a Prince. He's part Scotch collie remember," Frank said. "Bobbie would be a name you'd hear on the highlands of Scotland. I think it fits."

"Whatever the rest of you decide is fine by me," said Elizabeth.

Leona gave a little frown, but then shrugged her shoulders. "Well, if you both want Bobbie, it doesn't really matter to me. He's just a dog after all," she said.

So Nova won out, and I became Bobbie.

The day I met the Brazier's was the last day I saw my mother, dad, or brother. Everything happened so fast, I wasn't able to say goodbye. My last view of them was over the shoulder of Nova as she carried me away. Mother whimpered, but Dad was unusually quiet. They didn't have much say in the matter. I saw the sad, resigned look in their eyes, but I didn't fully understand what that meant for me.

5

Mr. Fiundt

I MUST HAVE SLEPT FOR SEVERAL HOURS, as the sun was low in the sky when I awoke. I looked around for the young man but did not see him. However, I did see another pan of food sitting on the steps of the porch, as well as a large basin of cool water. For the first time in a few days I was not hungry, but I ate the food anyway. Never turn your nose up to an easy meal.

I grabbed the bone and headed toward the street. Just as I was rounding the front side of the house, I saw the young man coming down the sidewalk with an armload of parcels. He stopped and gave me a big grin.

"Well, now! Where do you think you're off to? Are you going to eat and run? I thought you might like to stay for a while," he said.

I held my head down and my tail between my legs. The tone of his voice made me feel as if I had done something wrong.

"I think you need to stay around for a few days until you have had a few good meals. It'll give me time to find your owners," he said. "Come on in the house. It's getting late. You don't want to be on the road at night. I have a nice blanket for you to sleep on. I'll even let you bring that nasty old bone in the house with you."

I followed him into the house, but I kept one eye on the door. He left it open, which I thought was a good sign. I lay down on the rag rug by the door and spent the rest of the evening dozing, while the man sat in his chair and did something called a crossword puzzle. He listened to music on the radio. Frank and Elizabeth had a radio back in Silverton. It reminded me of them. Tomorrow I would start looking. As I fell asleep I heard a familiar song on the radio. "Yes, we have no bananas, we have no bananas today…"

Over the next few days, I stayed with the man, ate regular meals, rested up, and the two of us got along well.

During the day, he took me to the hardware store where he worked. I stayed behind the counter while he waited on his customers.

One day a pretty young woman came in with her father.

"Good morning, Mr. Fiundt. How are you today?" she said.

"G-good morning, M-Miss Sunderland. Mr. S-Sunderland. How can I help you?" Mr. Fiundt. (I'd noticed that whenever Mr. Fiundt was around other people he faltered in his speech. However, this was not the case when he talked directly to me.)

"Morning, Mr. Fiundt, can you tell me where you keep your fencing nails?" the older man said.

"They're along the b-b-back wall with the other b-bins of nails. Do you want me to s-show you, Mr. S-Sunderland?" Mr. Fiundt said.

"No, no, I'll find what I need," Mr. Sunderland said.

"Mr. Fiundt, where'd you get that adorable dog?" the young woman asked.

"P-Poor guy showed up at my b-back door half-starved. Don't s-suppose you have seen him before, Miss Sunderland?" Mr. Fiundt said.

"No, I don't know him," she said. "Dad, don't the Steingards, out on Germantown Road, have a collie-type dog?"

"Yea, but theirs is much darker. I've never seen this dog," Mr. Sunderland said.

"I am t-trying to find his owners. He sure is a great d-dog. He knows how to shake hands and s-speak. He follows close behind. He does have some odd habits though. He's so restless. He p-paces up and down the room. He's always going to the door or the window, like he's looking for someone," Mr. Fiundt said.

Miss Sunderland bent down to pet me.

"He sure has a sweet face. Oh, my, aren't we friendly. How do you do! Poor fellow. Maybe he misses his owner," she said.

"That's what I thought. But if no one claims him, I just m-might keep him. I haven't had a d-dog since I was a kid. Kind of miss having one around," Mr. Fiundt said.

"Why, Mr. Fiundt, I had no idea you were so soft-hearted. I think it's perfectly sweet that you are looking after him," Miss Sunderland said.

Mr. Fiundt turned various shades of red at her remarks.

"It's nothing r-really. I have a big house and it's felt kind of empty since my m-mother passed away. Trouble is I don't know that much about dogs. I don't know what they like to eat or what to do if they get sick..." Mr. Fiundt said.

"Why, we've had lots of dogs. I would be glad to help you. I just adore dogs. Maybe I could come by sometime and give you some pointers," Miss Sunderland said.

"T-that w-would be awfully nice of you. If you're sure it wouldn't be too much t-trouble," he said.

"It wouldn't be any trouble at all. I'd love to help out. Well, then it's all settled. I'll be in touch soon. In the meantime, just feed him lean-cooked meat, beef or chicken is all right. No bones though. I have a recipe our dogs really like. They seem to thrive on it. I'll bring that by. I'll look forward to seeing you and your new friend," she said scratching my ear.

"M-me too. And thanks, M-Miss S-Sunderland," he said.

Mr. Fiundt had a huge smile on his face as he watched Miss Sunderland and her father leave the store. He looked down at me.

"Thanks, fella," he said.

I wasn't sure what he was thanking me for, but he seemed happy and I wagged my tail.

⚓

Despite Mr. Fiundt's kindness, and the fact that I was getting attached to him, I decided it was time to move on. One morning, after breakfast, I scratched at the door to go outside. He shuffled to the door and held it open for me. As I stepped out, I gave him one last look. His hair was falling over his sleepy eyes.

"What is it, boy?" he said with furrowed eyebrows and a frown on his face. I think he knew. I turned and headed toward the road without looking back.

What direction I was going, I still did not know. I just followed the road out of town.

All I knew was that I must find my family. I had wasted enough time.

6

Tramp Dog

A FEW DAYS LATER, I came to a place called Crooked Lake where I found a tourist camp. As usual, I searched for Frank and Elizabeth, but I found no traces of them or their scent.

I cozied in with some vacationers for a while, but I didn't attach myself to anyone, and moved on after a day or so.

For days, I searched rest stops, campsites, and service stations. I traveled from town to town until one day when I came to a wide river on the edge of a large city.

Huddled around a campfire on the opposite shore were some men cooking food in a large, blackened pot. Even from across the river I could smell meat, and it drove me wild with hunger. Throwing caution to the wind, I swam the river. I had always been a strong swimmer. I proved that one day when I rescued Betsy from drowning in the Abiqua River back home. This river was wider than the Abiqua, and the current was stronger than I expected. When I came out on the other side, I was soaking wet and exhausted. I crawled, as close to the campfire as I felt was reasonably safe to do so.

A scruffy-looking man who smelled of wood smoke and cooking wine stared at me with his mouth hung open.

"Hey, Tom, did you see that dog swim the river? He must be pretty dang hungry to risk drowning. Why don't you give the poor fella some of that mulligan stew?" he said.

Tom, who looked as if he didn't get enough to eat as it was, dished out some of the savory-smelling stew onto a tin plate for me, then crumbled some crackers on top as well. It was the best-tasting mess I'd had in a long time. Despite its heat, I gulped it down, and gave a wag of the tail and a sharp bark to show my appreciation.

"Looks like this guy has been on the road for some time. A regular tramp dog. What do you say fella? All on your own?" Tom asked as he tossed me a few more crackers.

"I wonder where he came from. He's not a bad-looking dog. He's got a collar on him, so he belongs to somebody or used to. He doesn't look skinny enough to have been on the road for very long. But his coat is sure dirty and matted," Jim said.

"He looks strong. Probably a good watchdog. Collies are hard working and smart. I wonder where he came from? Well, welcome to Indianapolis, dog," Tom said.

These men were not the best-smelling people I ever encountered, but they were as good to me as any. Tom spread an old blanket for me by the fire. I slept next to him under the stars with the hum of the city around me. Occasionally, a long wail of a train whistle or the chug of a boat on the river would pierce the quiet. During the night, the men coughed, snored, and talked in their sleep. One of them must have been chasing rabbits for all the twitching and grunts he made. Despite all the strange smells and sounds, I was so tired that I had no trouble falling asleep.

7

Indianapolis

I WOKE TO THE SQUEALING AND CRUNCHING of trains on the freight yard not too far from our camp by the river. It was morning and the air was thick with a mist that settled on top of us in fine, cool droplets. Tom was the first awake but didn't seem in a hurry to leave his bedroll. Eventually he crept out, and the first thing he did was to start a fire to warm up by. As he poked the fire to life, he mumbled to himself in words I couldn't understand. I don't think he was directing his remarks to me. He continued to ramble on as he walked down to the river to fill a pan with water, which he then nestled next to the fire. When the water was warm, he lathered soap on his face and quickly ran a razor over his chin. Afterward, he fried up some fatty bacon that he placed between some cold biscuits he'd made the night before.

By this time, the other men were stirring from their bedrolls and grateful someone else started a fire. The smell of the bubbling bacon awakened my hunger, and I stayed close to the pan as each man in turn cooked his portion and shared some with me. I had never been a picky eater, and I wasn't going to start now. I don't think there was a man among them that didn't toss me something.

"Feeling a little better fella? Nothing like a warm fire and somethin' to fill your belly to lift your spirits, huh? How long you've been on the road fella?" Tom said in a voice as rough as his hands. "You and I are a

pair of bindle stiffs, hey boy. A couple of Joe Zilches, independent businessmen," he said giving me a big, toothless grin.

I wagged my tail, even though I didn't know what he was talking
about. But by the tone of his voice, I knew he was having fun with me.

All day, I stuck to Tom like skunk to a hound. I followed him around
town as he worked odd jobs that paid in cash or meals. At one house,
he raked leaves and burned trash. At a warehouse, he loaded wagons
and trucks. At the end of the day, he had some scratch in his pocket for
a hunk of bologna and a bottle of what he called "giggle water."

Later, by the campfire, Tom brought out his harmonica and sere-
naded the other campers. Whatever human invented this instrument
should have his ears cropped. I have never known a more annoying
sound. I tried to interrupt his recital, but my howling only encouraged
him. He continued to torture me to the amusement of the other
campers. As the night wore on, and as he sipped at his bottle, Tom
became more talkative.

"I remember when I was kid, living on my grandpa's farm in Wiscon-
sin. I had a dog named Jake. He went with me everywhere. Except
school. I sure loved that dog. Taught him all kinds of tricks. He knew
how to roll over and play dead. He was the best friend I ever had. It
broke my heart when my gramps had to put him down. I bawled like a
little schoolgirl," Tom said.

"Dogs are better than most people, if you ask me. Never met one
that didn't bite you unless he had a damn good reason. Unlike people,
who'll double-cross ya or give you the bum's rush for no reason whatso-
ever," Jim said.

"Ya got that straight. Hey, give me one them ciggys. Most people
wouldn't give ya the time of day. But I bet you that dog would lay down
his life for you or me and not even blink. It don't matter to him we ain't
got a roof over our heads or that we don't wear swanky clothes. You
could beat that dog to within an inch of his life and he'll still be your
pal. Heck, I'd trust him before I'd trust you, HA!" Tom said.

"That goes ditto for me, buster," Tom said.

The two men talked on through the night. As the fire died down, and
the night grew silent, I fell into a deep sleep and dreamt of my life on
the farm.

8
Working Dog

I HAD SAT ON NOVA'S LAP as we drove up the circular gravel drive beneath a canopy of budding oak trees toward my new home, a small farm on the Abiqua River outside of Silverton, Oregon. At the end of the drive I spotted a simple, white, two-story house and a small, weathered barn out back. Behind the barn was a large, fenced pasture area, where an old bronze-red horse was grazing.

On the front porch of the house was a little white fox terrier lying on a blanket in the pale sunshine. As we approached, his head popped up and he yapped a greeting. I stumbled up the steps as fast as my short legs would take me. We touched noses, and I sniffed his rear politely, but the little dog did not get up and do the same. He simply gave me a toothy grin and a wag of his stubby tail.

When he tried to get up, his rear legs gave out and remained limp behind him.

"Bobbie, this is Toodles. I just know you are going to be good friends. Toodles, this is Bobbie, your new brother. Now, Bobbie, you have to be gentle with Toodles. He's almost fourteen years old and has a bad heart. You have to play carefully with him," Nova said as she bounded up the steps.

I didn't understand. I looked at Toodles and gave him a couple of yaps to get him to play, but he didn't budge. I yanked on the blanket until it moved a few feet across the porch, but Toodles just sat and grinned. I yapped in frustration.

"Bobbie, he can't play with you. Leave him alone. You'll have plenty of playmates. There's a lot to do around here, Bobbie," Nova said.

She wasn't exaggerating. My first few weeks on the farm were busy ones. I practiced my herding skills on the Brazier's cats and chickens. I discovered the thrill of sticking my head down gopher holes.

Toodles followed me and hobbled for short distances around the farm, yapping his encouragement. On his bad days, when he couldn't walk at all, I dragged him around on his blanket. He never got cross or angry, and always had that odd, toothy grin. We became more than playmates, we became friends. More often than not, we could be found napping together on the front porch.

After a few months on the farm, I grew in length, size, and awkwardness. There was a brief time when my rear end refused to move in alignment with my front, and I walked with a list. Then, almost overnight, things turned around and I found my stride. I knew that my parents were with me in my heart and bones.

My earliest responsibility on the farm was moving the Brazier's Holsteins from the pasture for milking. I handled this as smoothly as butter on toast, if I do say so myself. Every morning, before Leona and Nova stumbled out of bed, I was already worrying the cows into the barn. Frank followed shortly after, and the girls after that.

Once the cows were in their stalls, the girls began the milking. They sat on wooden fruit crates and tugged at the cow's rubbery udders until a stream of milk squirted into the pail. Leona's face was puffy from sleep and she worked in silence, while Nova hummed cheerfully to herself. I wandered in and out of the stalls sniffing in the hay for roaming field mice.

"Bobbie, would you please get away from Salt and Pepper. You're making her nervous. It's hard enough to get a grip on her," Leona said.

"Salt and Pepper isn't nervous because of Bobbie, Leona. It's because you're in your usual bad mood," Nova said.

"Well, Bobbie doesn't help by coming up behind her. Go on Bobbie, get out of here," she said as she squirted me with an udder. I moved out of range and came around to where Nova was milking Pansy.

"Come here Bobbie. Leona is an old sourpuss. Besides, it's not you she's worried about. She won't admit it, but she's afraid of Salt and Pepper. Come over here, Bobbie. Sing with me! 'Yes, we have no bananas! We have no bananas today!'"

Nova's voice echoed off the walls of the barn, startling the mourning doves from the rafters. As they fluttered about, their wings made soft whistling sounds and sent a shower of feathers down on us.

Leona made a face at Nova's slightly off-key singing, but forced back a smile and shook her head.

As Leona and Nova finished the milking, I followed Frank around as he filled the feed bins with fresh hay and replenished the water.

He then led our horse, Ginger, out of her stall to release her into the pasture. However, she was more interested in the new alfalfa and refused to budge. Ginger was a retired Davenport Arabian, and she never let us forget that fact. To say she was headstrong would be an understatement. I decided to coax her along by coming up behind. However, at the same moment, she lashed out with her rear hoof and kicked me soundly in the head, which sent me flying to the back of the stall.

"Bobbie, are you all right?" Nova cried as she came running over.

"Oh my, look at the gash in his forehead. It's awfully deep. We better get that cleaned up."

She found a clean rag and dabbed at the cut above my right eye.

"Bobbie, you do have a knack for being in the wrong place at the wrong time. Do you think he needs stitches?" she said.

Frank looked at the wound above my eye.

"I think he'll be all right, but I'll have your mother take a look at it," he said.

"I told you he makes the animals nervous," Leona said. "If he had any sense, he would know to stay out of the way."

"He's still a pup and doesn't know better," Nova said. "But I bet he'll think twice about coming up behind Ginger again. Won't you Bobbie?"

After Nova cleaned my wound and the milk cans were stored in the cool, stone milk shed, we returned to the house for breakfast.

In the meantime, Elizabeth was bustling about the kitchen preparing the morning meal. There were stacks of thick, fluffy pancakes, rashers of crisp bacon, mounds of potatoes, eggs scrambled and fried and, of course, fresh milk. Everyone sat down at the large, green kitchen table and helped themselves.

Elizabeth examined the cut above my eye.

"I don't think he'll need stitches, but I better put some iodine on that cut. I bet he'll have a scar above that eye," she said.

Iodine was a horrible, smelly liquid that only made it sting all the more. When she finished cleaning my wound, she fed Toodles and me in the pantry off the kitchen, as Elizabeth would not allow us at the table during meals. She gave me a slightly larger portion than usual for my sorrows. From the pantry, with the door ajar, I could hear the morning's conversation.

"You know, Elizabeth, with all this hard work we've been doing, I can eat anything I want and not gain weight. I feel fit as a fiddle," Frank said ladling a pile of potatoes onto his plate.

"I think your cough has improved too, Frank, despite your 'occasional' cigar," Elizabeth said. "Moving to Oregon was just what you needed. I think it's done us all some good. Just look at those rosy cheeks on Leona and Nova."

"My cheeks are red because I'm hot. It's hard work lugging all those cans to the milk shed. I wouldn't mind so much if it weren't so early in the morning," Leona said as she snatched some bacon off the platter.

"Frank, dear, why don't you have a talk with the cows? See if they can move the milking up to noon, so Leona can sleep in," Elizabeth said.

"I love to get up early, especially in the spring when the days get longer. The morning is always so fresh and full of promise. I can't help but wonder what the day will bring," Nova said.

"We are all fully aware that you are a morning bird, Nova. You don't need to remind us," Leona said with a twisted smile.

"Leona dear, what do you and Clifton have planned for Saturday night?" Elizabeth said as she set a tower of toast on the table.

"There's a program at the Palace we thought we would go to. There's going to be music and some recitations," Leona said. "I thought I would wear the dress you finished hemming for me Mother, the dark-blue one with the white-lace collar."

"Oh, that looks so nice on you, Leona. Especially when you have your hair loose around your shoulders," Elizabeth said.

"Don't you think Leona would look nice with bobbed hair, Mother?" Nova said. "It's so thick and wavy."

"I don't know. I think one girl with bobbed hair is enough for this family," Elizabeth said.

"Clifton doesn't like bobbed hair anyway. He doesn't think it's feminine," Leona said. "It looks ok on you Nova. You're such a tomboy anyway. But I don't think I would feel right with my hair so short."

"I think you would look very chic with it bobbed. All the movie stars are wearing their hair that way. At least let me help you fix it differently for Saturday night. You always have it pulled back so tight. We could soften it up a little and add a few curls around the face," Nova said.

"Well, it might be fun to try something new, as long as it's not too extreme," Leona said.

"Nova, do you have any plans with that nice Garver boy this weekend?" Elizabeth asked.

"He and I are not on speaking terms at the moment," Nova said with a frown on her face. "If he thinks he can wait until the last minute before he asks me out, he is mistaken. I just may see the new Valentino movie without him," she said.

"I'm not so sure I want my youngest daughter going to a Rudolf Valentino movie unchaperoned. I heard this new one is even more exotic than the last one," Elizabeth said.

"But mother, Rudy Valentino is the bees-knees. If I can't see his new movie, I'll be the only one who hasn't. Besides, I won't go alone. I'll ask Frances Doerfler," Nova said.

"I thought Frances was seeing that Billy Gable? Won't she be going with him?" Leona said.

"Oh, they aren't serious. Billy Gable flirts with all the girls. He's even flirted with me at the Cunningham's Confectionery. I heard that he only plans to work at the mill for a couple of years and then go to California. Frances has more sense than to get attached to one of the roving types," Nova said.

"Now, some of the men from the mill are nice, stable types. However, a few spend too much time at Mac's Place, if you ask me. Why don't you and Frances wait until a Mary Pickford picture comes to town? She's such a lovely, wholesome actress. You are awfully young to see a Rudolf Valentino picture," Elizabeth said shaking her head.

"But Mother, you let me see *The Sheik*", Nova said.

"That's because I didn't know what it was about. I swear these Hollywood people push the limits of propriety," Elizabeth said. "They fill a young girl's head with all these romantic notions. It's no wonder a nice Silverton boy isn't good enough for you, Nova."

"It's not that Silverton boys aren't good enough for me, it's just that they're so unsophisticated. I'd rather go out with...Buster Keaton than with some of them," Nova said.

"Well, if you are going to be so choosy, then Buster Keaton is who you will end up with," Leona said.

"Well, then, call me Mrs. Keaton," Nova said.

"Now, now you two, let's get through breakfast without arguing," Frank said. "I suppose it's natural for young girls to want to see pictures with a handsome leading-man such as Rudy Valentino, but give me a Buster Keaton movie any day. The stunts that guy does! I can't stop laughing. His body must be made of rubber. Yet, his face never changes expression," Frank said.

"Frank, Buster Keaton may be funny, but he's not exactly a dream come true in the looks department. Although, I would rather have Nova go to one of his movies instead of one of Valentino's," Elizabeth said.

Nova rolled her eyes but ate her breakfast in silence.

"Leona, dear, after breakfast I could use your help in the kitchen. I want to put some new shelf paper up and we need to empty the cupboards before I do that," Elizabeth said.

"Yes, Mother. Whatever you say," Leona said.

"Nova, you better finish your breakfast and get ready for school," Elizabeth said. Nova hurriedly ate the remainder of her breakfast and then washed up. On her way out the door, she gave me a gentle rub on my chest.

"Stay out of mischief, Bobbie. At least, for the rest of the day," she said.

Just as quickly as they had all assembled, the table now became empty. Elizabeth cleared the dishes and scraped the leftovers into the garbage bin. Why they didn't bury their food to save for later, I never figured out.

Frank lingered at the table a little longer, doing what he called his paperwork. Elizabeth emptied cupboards, as Leona washed the morning dishes.

I finished my breakfast and licked Toodles' plate clean as well.

Frank looked over at me, laughed, and shook his head.

"Trouble follows you like a shadow, doesn't it Bobbie! I hope you learned your lesson for today," he said.

I sure did. Stay clear of the east end of a westbound horse.

9

The Hobo Life

*L*IFE WITH TOM was anything but routine. Most of the time he wandered around town like he was lost, always muttering to himself. Still, he watched over me, and I watched over him. At night, I slept by his side, and if anyone came too close, I let them know.

Even though we lived in the open and our meals weren't regular, I got used to his ways. But I still missed my family and grew restless. As we walked around the city, I was always on the lookout for them. Every time I heard an automobile horn, I looked to see if it was the Overland.

"What's the matter boy? Scared of car horns? Or do you want to go for a ride?" Tom said.

I barked at the mention of a ride.

"So it is a ride. You must have had it swell. Taking rides in cars. Guess you kind of look down on all this walking around, huh?" he said as he ruffled my fur.

Sometimes, when Tom was working, I wandered off by myself to search for my family. I checked out the usual tourist camps and service stations. Finally, after a week or so of fairly regular meals and rest, I decided to move on.

One morning, before Tom awoke and lit the fire, I made my move. I gave him one last look, as he lay tucked into his bedroll with a tuft of gray hair sticking out. He would be all right. He had the rest of his pack to look after him. He wouldn't miss me.

I found the main road out of town and took it. When I was a few miles away from the city, I climbed to the top of a hill to get my bearings. All around me were fields of pale, yellow corn stalks. As the fog lifted, the sun broke through and I closed my eyes against its brightness. I remembered the sun had been in my eyes every morning on our trip to Indiana, just as it was today. I realized then, that home to Oregon would be in the opposite direction. That meant if I went away from the morning sun, I should be going in the direction of home. I decided then that is what I should do—head west.

First, I needed to find the road that we took to Indiana. I headed in a north-westerly direction, as that seemed the right way to go.

From the long stretches of road through the countryside, I saw workers in the fields picking corn and soybeans. I thought back to when I was with my family in the orchards and hop fields at harvest time, back in my beloved Silverton.

10

Harvest Time

ONE MORNING, IN LATE AUGUST, Frank, Elizabeth, Nova, and Leona boarded trucks and wagons with other pickers and drove out to the hop fields for harvesting. I came along, as it was my job to watch over the children.

Leona and Nova worked side by side picking the hops. However, Leona didn't enjoy harvesting any better than she did the milking.

"It's so hot. I wish I'd remembered my hat. Now I'm going to get all sunburned. I feel like I've been cooking for hours over a hot stove," she said.

She plopped down on the ground and pulled out her handkerchief to wipe her forehead and neck.

"Gosh, I hate the out-of-doors. Picking hops is so messy and dusty. The leaves are so scratchy, my fingers are chaffed," she said.

"We're all hot and tired, Leona. If you spent more time picking than you did complaining, you'd get more work done. Besides, it helps if you wear gloves or wrap your fingers with cloth tape," Nova said as she reached under the fuzzy leaves, carefully snapped a flower cluster, and dropped it into a large, cone-shaped basket.

"I'm just not cut out for this kind of work. After Clifton and I get married, I hope I never step in another hop field in my life," Leona said.

Nova worked quietly for a while, but then looked off into the distance as if thinking of something else.

"Leona, don't you feel as if you are missing out on something by getting married. Don't you want to see something of the world outside of Silverton? I could never marry and settle down without seeing Paris or London. There is so much out there to experience," she said.

"Well, maybe someday, after we're married, Clifton and I will travel. But, in the meantime, I'm happy right here in Silverton," Leona said.

"Well, my life isn't all planned out like yours. Sometimes I know what I want to do, but it all seems so out of reach. It's just not fair. It's expected that girls get married right out of school. If you aren't married by the time you're twenty, people start to wonder about you. You're a pitiful creature that everyone whispers about and feels sorry for. If you're a boy, you're considered eligible until your old and fat. Sometimes, I wish I were a boy. Then I could do anything I want," Nova said.

"Life isn't without some responsibilities, Nova, even for boys. Look at Clifton. He could have left Silverton and explored the world. But no, he started his own business. And he's very successful. Why, I bet he just might be mayor some day. He may not be as exciting as Rudolf Valentino, but he has a solid future ahead of him," Leona said.

"There's more to life besides a solid future. What about music, art, books, and travel? Those are the things I want to experience," Nova said.

"Well, you can dream all you want, but that doesn't mean it's going to come true. Once you finally get serious with a boy, your attitude will change. You'll see," Leona said.

The girls worked in silence, establishing a quiet rhythm to their picking. I returned to the end of the row where the younger children were playing. We kept them in a group so I could keep an eye on them. At first, everything seemed as it should be. I spotted a rabbit peeking out among the vines and chased after it. It criss-crossed several times through the hop poles and I lost track of it. I was nosing around for its scent trail when I heard the yells of several of the children. I came out from beneath the canopy of leaves to see what was going on.

A little blond boy ran up to Leona and Nova crying.

"Ethel is missing. She must have crawled away when we weren't looking. I didn't mean to lose her. We were chasing rabbits like Bobbie. Then she was gone. I'm sorry," he said smearing the tears from his grimy face.

All the adults within earshot came running to see what the commotion was about. The little boy pointed to where he had last seen Ethel. They all spread out calling out Ethel's name.

"You girls check the hop swales," Frank said. "The rest of you better check the irrigation ditches."

Ethel's mother started to cry at the mention of the ditches.

"Oh, my God, she wouldn't have gone that far. Would she? She's only been walking for a few weeks," she said looking at the other women.

"I'm sure she couldn't have gone far. She'll be all right. We'll find her. Don't you worry," Elizabeth said with her arm around the mother.

I came back to the spot where little Ethel was last playing. I easily found her talcum-laced scent and followed it to a patch of blackberry brambles not far from the road. Her trail became stronger as I approached. I knew she was somewhere in the mess of thorny vines. People don't know how to use the nose in front of their face. I barked to get their attention.

"Over there, Bobbie's found something," Frank said.

They all came near and peered in and around the brambles.

"Ethel, Ethel, honey. Are you in there? It's time to come out now," her mother cried out.

Several others called out Ethel's name. After a moment of silence, Ethel squealed from the middle of the vines.

"There she is. Somebody's got to go in there and get her," Ethel's mother said looking around. "Couldn't one of the smaller boys crawl under and pull her out?"

No one immediately volunteered. Meanwhile, Ethel's cries increased in volume.

"She must be hurt. Ethel, honey, it will be all right. Mommy's here," she said.

"Maybe if we got a machete, we could whack the vines down around her," one of the men suggested.

"Listen to her, she's scared to death. Can't someone just crawl in there and get her? Oh, you're all afraid of a few scratches. I'll do it myself," the mother said.

"Let me do it, Mrs. Johnson, I'm smaller than you and can get in there easier," Nova said.

While Nova turned down the sleeves of her dress and tightened the scarf around her hair, I took matters into my own paws. I followed Ethel's trail beneath the vines, heading toward the sound of her cries.

I could hear the others calling out.

"Bobbie, Bobbie, do you see her?" "Good boy, Bobbie. Good boy, find her, boy!" "Everything's going to be ok Ethel, honey."

"Even if he does find her, we still have to find a way to get her out," I heard Leona say.

Frank called over to one of the men.

"Why don't you get that machete. We could start cutting down some of these vines, while Bobbie pins her down," he said.

I snaked my way around the toughest of the vines, crawling on my belly at times to reach Ethel. I finally spotted her beneath a woven cave of greenery. The back of her dress was snagged on a vine. Other than a few angry scratches on her neck and berry stains all over, she was in one piece. I ran up to her and gave her face a good licking and she immediately stopped crying. I barked to let everyone know that I had found her.

"He's found her! He's found her!" Mrs. Johnson said.

I grabbed the back of Ethel's dress with my mouth and yanked it free from the vine. She quickly waddled off. Taking care to find openings around the sharp thorns, I nudged her in the right direction toward the edge and barked at intervals to let the others know where we were. Soon we found the small clearing they had created with the machete. When Ethel emerged from the patch, her mother scooped her up in her arms, held her close, and covered her face in kisses. Elizabeth came over and made a quick examination.

"Poor little thing! She must have been scared. What a mess she is. Those are some nasty scratches on her neck. Leona, would you get the witch hazel from the medical kit. We better get her cleaned up," Elizabeth said.

Several people gave me a pat on the head and said, "Good boy!" Soon everyone returned to work. Only Nova and Leona remained behind with me.

Nova knelt down and hugged me around the neck. With a soft whisper to my ear she said, "You're a good boy, Bobbie, a good boy. I am very proud of you." She looked into my eyes and held my head with her small hands.

"You're a lot smarter than most people give you credit for," she said.

Leona looked at me with a crooked smile and said, "Not so bad, Bobbie. You might turn out all right after all."

Later, as I walked by Frank, he just stood there and looked down at me as if seeing me for the first time. Then, he gave me a gentle pat on the head, a slight smile on his face.

"Well, Bobbie, as Nova would say, 'You're the cat's meow!'" he said. That was all the reward I needed.

11

Tippecanoe & Bobbie Too!

THE NOISE AND CONGESTION of Indianapolis were days behind me, but I still had not found the right road toward home. With new determination, I followed my hunch, kept the pale morning sun to my right, and headed in a north-westerly direction. I just knew that this should get me to the route we had come east on.

I scrounged for meals behind the houses and businesses of the towns I passed through. Sometimes strangers tossed me a bone or a scrap from the family's dinner. I didn't look down my nose on anything. Beggars can't be choosers.

I crossed one major river by way of a train trestle. The next river was a smaller, slower-moving river, which I swam across. I later found out it was called the Tippecanoe River. On the opposite shore, I spotted a tourist camp. The place was nearly deserted, except for some people camping beneath the trees and in the cabins lining the river.

On the lawn in front of one of the cabins was a white-haired woman sitting in a wicker chair. She was husking ears of corn. She spotted me and called out, but I was more interested in checking out the rest of the camp. Therefore, I moved on.

For days I circled the area, checking all the cabins and campsites along the river. The same woman spotted me several times, and each time she called out to me. Finally, I cautiously approached her as she sat in a chair beneath a large willow.

"Well, there fellow, are you finally going to come and say hello? Are you lost? There was a man looking for a collie dog just the other day. Do you belong to him? He called his dog 'Bobbie.' Could you be his Bobbie?" she asked.

At the mention of my name, I wagged my tail and came closer.

"Well, you know your name, that's for sure. Don't you Bobbie? You look as if you have been on the road for a while. It doesn't seem possible to me that you could be this same man's Bobbie. He had just lost his dog and you look like you've been lost for some time. You look hungry. Would you like something to eat?" she asked me.

At the mention of food, I wagged my tail even more, perked up my ears, and did a few quick circles. I found this always worked when it came to getting their attention. The woman slowly got out of her rocking chair and walked into the cottage. A few minutes later, she came out with some fatty end-pieces of steaks. While I chewed the fat with the woman, a few more people came out of the cottage.

"So this is the dog you were talking about, Sarah," a short, round man said. "He seems to be enjoying that steak well enough. He must be hungry. He does look a little scrawny. Look at his coat. It hasn't been brushed in awhile. He'd be a good-looking dog all cleaned up and with a little meat on his bones. Ha! Ha! Meat on his bones, get it?"

The little man laughed so hard at his own joke he gave a little snort. I looked at him strangely, for I had never heard a human snort before.

"Oh, George, even the dog thinks that's a bad joke," Sarah said. "Why don't you get me one of our old brushes and let's see if we can spruce him up a bit. He's got a nice leather collar on him but no name plate or tag. He seems to answer to the name of 'Bobbie.' Wasn't that the name of the dog that man was looking for the other day? I wonder if this is his dog. We should check at the camp office to see if the man left his name and address. He sure is a friendly fellow and so polite. He shook my hand when he first came up to me."

"Are you sure he didn't give you his paw for a handout?" George asked. "Dogs have a way of worming food out of people," he said eyeing me suspiciously.

"I don't care. He looked hungry, so I gave him some food. You're not any worse for it," Sarah said as she poked George in the stomach.

George smiled, but his cheeks turned a little red, and he held himself erect as he made an effort to pull his stomach in. "What do you think we should do with this 'Bobbie?'" he said.

"I think we should see about that man at the camp office first. There's no harm in keeping him around for a while and feeding him until we find out about his owner. He's such a well-mannered dog. He can't be too much trouble. When I first saw him, he wouldn't come to me. He seemed to be looking for someone and in such a hurry. Maybe that man was his owner or just some other tourist driving through. It probably happens quite often, dogs getting lost from their owners. It seems to me that if you are traveling with a dog you should put some sort of name on the collar so that people can contact you if the dog gets lost. As far as we know this Bobbie could have come as far as New York or California. Or he could live down the road from here. We probably will never know. Don't you worry, Bobbie, I'll take care of you while you're here," Sarah said.

I gave her one of my best whimpers and a quick flick of the tongue.

"Here we go again! If I had a wooden nickel for every animal you've taken in, I'd be a rich man," George said.

Over the next few days, I searched the campground, rested, and ate regular meals. Still, there was no sign of my family. The Pratt family checked at the office for any messages regarding a lost dog and found there was none. This news seemed to please Mrs. Pratt, and she made even more fuss over me than before. She smelled like Nova. How I missed her.

12

Bosom Buddies

*I*N BETWEEN CHORES, Nova and I escaped as often as possible and explored the back roads around the farm.

One day, while everyone else was out of the house, Nova packed a lunch of chicken sandwiches, potato salad, and some of Elizabeth's apple strudel into a basket, and strapped it to the back of her bicycle. With me running alongside, she followed the road to the Abiqua River where we came to a covered bridge shaped like a barn. Nova leaned her bicycle against the railing at the entrance and stood looking down the road past the rows of hop vines. Off in the distance I could see the great hill of Mount Angel pushing up out of the valley floor. There was no one else about, and the only sound was that of the water trickling beneath the bridge, and the peaceful trill of red-winged blackbirds among the reeds.

Nova waited for a while at one end of the bridge, but then started pacing back and forth across the broad, wooden planks. I passed the time by barking at the pigeons in the rafters of the bridge.

"Bobbie, be quiet now! You're giving me a headache!" Nova said as she peered down the road. Her face had that pinched "I am not pleased" look. I thought it best to stay out of her way, so I climbed down the embankment to splash around in the river and worry some ducks.

Down the road, I spotted the Crockett boys with their fishing poles heading toward the bridge. As they approached, one of them pointed to Nova's basket on the back of her bicycle.

"Hey, Nova, goin' on a picnic for one? Looks like someone's been stood up!" he called out.

"Just mind your own business, Ed Crockett," Nova said. "Take your scabby knees and smelly fish and go away."

"This bridge is for everyone to use, not just for those looking for some smooching. If you need a kiss, I'm available!" he said smacking his lips together.

"No, thank you, I'd rather kiss one of those fish," she said.

The boys laughed and moved on down the road.

After awhile, William Garver came by on his bicycle and stopped when he reached Nova. She had her hands on her hips and a frown on her face. She started yelling the minute she saw him, her voice echoing off the walls of the bridge and drifting down the road.

The whole encounter ended with her throwing plums at William as he sped off on his bicycle.

Nova cried as she jumped on her bicycle and pedaled furiously in the opposite direction toward Mount Angel. I could hardly keep up with her. After awhile, we reached the base of the hill and climbed to the top where the abbey overlooks the valley. By then Nova was out of breath, but not out of tears. She found a bench beneath some trees where she sat down and cried some more. In between intermittent sobs, she unpacked her lunch and ate her picnic. As she stared off into the distance, she broke off little pieces of her extra sandwich and fed them to me.

I have found that people often do things I don't understand. I didn't know why Nova was crying, but I knew something was not right. I put my head on her lap to remind her that she wasn't alone. She looked down at me with red, puffy eyes.

"Oh, Bobbie, you are always there for me, aren't you? I love you so much. I really do. Much more than some people. And I am not ashamed to say it. Leona thinks I'm crazy to love a dog so much. 'It's just not natural to carry on about a dog. Dogs are animals, not children,'" Nova said imitating Leona's whiney voice.

"I don't care. I love everything about you. I love your silky ears, how your fur glows all warm-red in the sun, and how you smell like the out-of-doors. I love your funny, little bobbin tail. No matter what, you always make me laugh. Like when you dig for gophers up to your elbows, and the way you tease Toodles. You're the only one I can really depend on. Certainly not boys. Why are they such a bother, Bobbie? I go to all the trouble of making a picnic lunch and that William Garver can't even show up on time. Then he tells me he isn't even hungry. I swear this is the last time I will ever go to the trouble. I don't ever want to see him again," she said.

She buried her face into the fur around my neck and cried some more. I licked the tears from her face, and she finally smiled.

The wind carried the sound of the bells from the church in town, along with the familiar smells of hops, raspberries, and the sheep on the Sigurdson's farm. My whole world was in that wind.

"Sometimes, Bobbie, when I am up here looking across the valley, I just ache inside to be somewhere beyond those mountains. When I hear the train whistle, I wish I could be one of the people on it, going somewhere. And yet, I love being here, Bobbie, especially with you. It makes me feel as if all my troubles are miles away. It's so beautiful and peaceful. Look, you can see Mount Hood today. And there's the Abiqua. That must be the Pudding River over there. How the water sparkles through the cottonwoods. I wish we could stay here on this hill forever, Bobbie. Just you and me," she said.

So do I.

Later, when we returned to the farm, Nova got into trouble with Elizabeth for being gone so long. Then, when Elizabeth found out that we'd been to the Gallon House Bridge, she had a few choice words for Nova.

"I don't know how many times I have told you to stay away from that area. There are bootleggers in that old house down there, and who knows what kind of riff-raff. Nice girls do not go on picnics at the Gallon House Bridge. I'll not have any daughter of mine be known as...a...FLAPPER! This is what happens when you let your daughter get her hair bobbed," Elizabeth sputtered, her cheeks red and her hair falling out of its pins.

"Jeepers creepers, Mother. We only went for a picnic, not to buy apple whiskey," Nova said.

    "I don't care what you were doing. You are not to go there again, ever," Elizabeth said with a punch to some dough rising in a bowl on the counter. I hid beneath the table as she ranted on and on. I nudged Nova's hand to remind her that I was there. She remained silent but rolled her eyes at me. This wasn't the first time, nor would it be the last, that Nova and I got into hot water with Elizabeth.

13

Westward Ho!

*A*FTER A FEW DAYS OF REST and regular meals with Mrs. Pratt and her family on the quiet shores of the Tippecanoe, I decided to move on. So one morning, before the sun rose and only a song sparrow broke the stillness of the camp, I crept off the front porch of the cabin past the rocking chair on the lawn where I had first spotted Mrs. Pratt and disappeared down the road.

After a couple of days, I came to a wide, paved road heading west. I knew there was only one road that had so many layers of odors. I knew that a great many people, automobiles, carts, and horses had been this way. Could it be the same? It smelled the same as the road that I remembered.

I looked around and realized I was not far from the town of Wolcott where I had originally gotten lost. I had been going in circles all this time! Now I only had to follow this road toward the setting sun, and that would lead me toward home.

I found a new rhythm now that I was heading in the right direction. As I trudged through the gently-rolling farmland, I began to notice the signs of the changing season. The grasses and weeds that lined the road were the same bleached yellow of the drying corn. The maples and birches were showing a hint of yellow and orange among the olive green leaves.

After several days, I came to the town of Peoria. As I walked down one of the residential streets, I came to the house where we had stayed the night with Elizabeth's friends. I remembered they were not very fond of dogs, and I had to spend the night on the porch watching the fireflies.

As I approached the house, the woman named Vivian came out to shake some rugs, and spotted me at the end of the sidewalk.

"Get out of here you mangy mongrel! Go on, get!"

Obviously, she didn't recognize me. And since there was no sign of Frank or Elizabeth, I left.

After a few days had passed and a number of miles, I came to the great river I had crossed with my family. "The Mississippi," Frank had called it. I remembered how wide and flat it was and how the patchwork of farmland faded into the horizon.

Like the road I was traveling on, the river was a mixture of smells, water, silt, fish, fuel, smoke, and dead things. Only the Mississippi smelled like the Mississippi. And only the Mississippi was as busy as any highway. There were tugboats pushing barges, paddle wheel boats spewing smoke and steam, and ships with masts and sails.

After sundown, under cover of darkness, I found the entrance to the bridge. A dense fog had risen from the river, and I was able to use this to my advantage. I heard water lapping up against supports beneath me, and the sound of men's voices echoing from inside a little room elevated above the bridge.

I remembered that Frank had grumbled about paying something called a toll to cross the bridge.

"Ten cents a car! And five cents for each passenger! This is highway robbery. The only way you fellows get away with it, is that there isn't another bridge for miles," he had said to the men in the booth.

I stayed in the shadows, held my head down, and kept close to the ground. A shaft of light emanated from the bridge tower. I waited until the men were not looking in my direction. Just as I was about to go past, the door flew open, and one of the men came out. I was still in the shadows and he didn't see me. He stood gazing about with a lantern in his hand.

"Ed, I'm going to make the rounds," he said.

The other man grunted in response. He headed down the walkway in the opposite direction from where I was hiding. I quietly followed him from a distance, staying out of the pool of light cast by his lantern.

At the end of the bridge he turned. I stood rock still. I wasn't sure what to do.

He then headed back in the other direction. I stayed low and slowly crawled away from the man on the opposite side. As I skulked by, he stopped and held up his lantern in my direction. I froze in my tracks and crouched to the ground. Luckily, a barrier of metal supports blocked his view of me.

"Anyone out there," he called out.

I was careful not to move until he was well past me. When the time was right, I took off like a jackrabbit.

Eventually, I came to the outskirts of the town of Burlington, where I recognized the large train roundhouse with its web of railroad tracks in all directions. I found an empty train car where I slept for a few hours. I moved on at dawn.

Every now and then, as I traveled, I would recognize a barn, a church steeple, or some other landmark that assured me I was on track.

I made good time now that I knew I was going in the right direction. I stopped only to scrounge for food, or to rest.

When I came to the town of Oskaloosa, I found the Shady Lawn tourist camp where my family and I stayed. I recognized the little cabins with the flower boxes and picket fences out front.

I remembered how, in the evening, we had sat at the picnic tables beneath the large oak trees. Elizabeth cooked dinner over the common fire pit, while Frank shared stories of their travels and made recommendations of places to see. I liked that part of the day as much as the changing scenery during the day. It was less dusty and bumpy. Children played with me. I met other dogs and we combed the campsite together, making our marks at strategic points. I've noticed that people do not find it necessary to mark their territory in the same way.

Later, some of the campers brought out instruments, including a harmonica, and played music as we sat around the campfire. To call what that instrument of torture produces "music" is a stretch of the imagination. I howled in protest, but Frank and Elizabeth only encouraged my vocalizations. Everyone found it very amusing. You would think they liked to see me suffer.

We huddled around the campfire until the stars came out, and the fire burned low. Eventually, everyone slipped away to their cabins and went to sleep.

As there was no sign of my family, I didn't stay long in Oskaloosa and moved on.

After a few days, I came to a fork in the road where I got sidetracked on a road to Vinton, Iowa. While I was there, I jumped into the car of a family named Patton. They took me home and fed me, but I only stayed one night. I left early the following morning before any feelings got hurt.

14

Des Moines

*I*FOLLOWED THE ROAD OUT OF VINTON until I came to the fork where I originally was sidetracked; I took the branch heading true west. The sun was at my back and the weather was mild. Before long, the countryside began to look familiar again. As I came to the outskirts of Des Moines, I spotted the large, white building with the glinting, golden dome on top that I remembered from the trip east.

Walking down the main street, I came to the river that cut the town in half, and to the same bridge my family had used to cross it.

I searched until after sunset for something to eat and a place to rest.

As I padded through the empty streets, the only sounds I heard were other dogs barking at me from the end of their chains. Eventually, I came to a large house set back from the main road. All was quiet. The screen door to the porch was unlatched, so I nosed it open and snuck inside.

Through the darkness, I saw a young man asleep on a cot at the end of the porch with his hand hanging down over the edge. I gave it a nudge with my nose and licked it. The boy woke up and blinked in surprise. He reached out and petted me on the chest. I lifted my paw to shake hands. He quietly stroked me until he fell asleep again. I laid down next to him on the porch floor and fell asleep as well.

In the morning, the sun was above the horizon when noises from inside the house woke me up. I could smell smoked meat cooking and my mouth began to water. The young man was still asleep, but he stirred beneath his blankets. When I nudged him with my nose, he threw his arm across his face and rolled over to go back to sleep. Then he opened his eyes as if he had remembered something. He turned over and gave me a sleepy smile through half-closed eyes.

"Hello, boy, so you stuck around, did you? I thought maybe you were a dream," he said.

He gave my head a gentle stroke and a little scratch behind the ear.

"Where did you come from? I've never seen you before. Are you lost? I bet you wandered over from the tourist camp down the road. Are you hungry? I know I am."

At the mention of food, I perked my ears up and gave him my most enthusiastic bark. As he stumbled barefoot into the house, I was about to follow him, but he told me to stay on the porch. I didn't want to press my luck, so I waited outside. He came out shortly with a bowl of milk and some pieces of bacon. Following behind were a white-haired man and woman, and another younger woman.

"Here he is, Aunt Ida," the boy said as he knelt down to give me the food. I ate the bacon in several swallows and followed it with the bowl of milk. After licking all the milk droplets that landed on the porch, I greeted everyone with a paw shake.

Aunt Ida offered me a pale, blue-veined hand. She was a small, thin woman who wore her hair in a bun behind her head. Flour and grease spots covered the large, cotton apron over her plain dress and smelled of the morning's breakfast. A few hairs had freed themselves from their pins and hung down over her smiling, red face.

"Well, hello there, boy. You sure are a spunky thing, letting yourself into other people's houses in the middle of the night," she said. "I think you are right, Freddy. He most likely wandered over from the tourist camp. Somebody's probably out looking for him right now. Why don't you go over there in a little while and do some asking around. His owners must be worried. He sure is a friendly fellow and so well behaved. He must come from a nice family."

After breakfast, Freddy walked me through the tourist camp, which I immediately recognized. *I remember Frank filling up on water at that pump over there.* I searched the faces and the automobiles inhabiting the camp and checked for any familiar scents, but I didn't find any. I marked everywhere so that they knew I had been there. Later, Freddy asked about me at the office, and left his name just in case anyone reported a missing dog.

The next day, I wandered through the camp by myself and did a more thorough search. For the most part, no one bothered me until I came to a campsite occupied by several adults and a number of noisy, smelly children of every shape and size.

An orange-haired boy with spots on his face and dirty hands and knees caught sight of me as I walked past.

"Hey look, a dog. Here doggie, dooogie! Here boy!" he called in a raspy, froggy voice. I tried to ignore him, but he ran after me, followed by a small, unkempt army of his kind. They all looked as if they could use a good licking.

"Hey, I was here first. Get outta the way, you! I want to pet him."

"Hey, watch yer elbows!"

"Yer full of baloney. I was here first. Wait yer turn."

The youngest clamped his sticky fists on to the fur around my neck and hung on. They all poked, prodded, probed, and rubbed me the wrong way.

When most of them had lost interest and moved onto other things, the orange-haired boy grabbed me by the collar and pulled me toward their campsite.

"Ma, Pa, look here. We found a dog. Can we keep him here?"

The mother was sitting in the shade. Parts of her bottom spilled out over the sides of the chair. She breathed heavily, and it seemed an effort just to speak.

"Well, just for a while. But we ain't takin' no stray dog with us on to Nebraska. You can play with him, but then send him on his way," she said.

"Aw, you don't know what you're talking about. Bring the dog over here!" the father said.

The man yanked me by the collar and looked me over, his face pressed close to mine. His breath smelled of fruit rotting in the sun.

"Humph. I bet I could get a good price for this dog. Tie him up over there by the car. And keep an eye on him if you know what's good for you," he said.

The boy took me over to the car where he removed my wide leather collar and replaced it with a shabby piece of leather shoelace. He then tied that to a length of rope that he attached to the back of the car.

"That'll hold you. Now stay there dog. I bet I could sell this collar," he said.

With all the commotion I did not notice, at first, the old female hound cowering beneath the automobile. I walked over to greet her but found my tether was too short. Eventually, she crawled out and hobbled toward me. As she came into the light, I could see that her ribs and backbone stuck out sharply against her brown, papery skin. There were fresh sores and old scars covering her body. Her dull eyes were suspicious of me. I gave her a friendly sniff. She gave me a feeble wag of her tail as she cowered to the ground. She rolled over on her back to let me know she meant no threat. She seemed afraid of her own shadow.

Whenever she heard yelling or a loud noise, she crawled beneath the automobile again where she spent most of her time chewing at the bald spots on her feet.

For the longest time, I stayed tied to the automobile. I pulled, yanked, and barked, but no one paid attention.

Toward evening, one of the little girls threw me some old bread, taking delight in throwing some pieces beyond my reach. That was all I had to eat for the rest of the night.

The family gathered around the campfire until late into the evening. At one point, the father and mother began to argue with each other. Their yelling echoed through the otherwise quiet campsite. I heard breaking glass and the clanging of kitchenware.

I barked frantically to get their attention, but then the father came over and gave me a swift kick in the ribs.

"Shut up you mangy mongrel, if you know what's good for ya," he said.

I yelped and scurried out of the way. Now I understood why the hound remained out of sight. I kept my mouth shut after that.

I waited until the last of the voices faded away and everyone was asleep. Then I chewed through the grimy rope and ran away, leaving that poor, worn out hound to her fate.

By the next morning, I returned to Aunt Ida's house. I figured she would be good for some T-bone and sympathy. Freddy greeted me like an old friend.

"Hey, boy, where have you been? What's this? What happened to your nice leather collar? Did somebody try to tie you up? It looks like you chewed right through the rope. What a clever fellow! They probably didn't feed you as well as we do. That's why you came back, isn't it? I think he likes us, Aunt Ida. Otherwise, why would he come back?" he said.

"Does seem kind of odd he would run off. Especially chewing through his rope like that. A dog that is well-loved and cared for would have no reason to run away. But, I think we need to give it a little more time before we make any decisions about keeping him," Aunt Ida said. "He sure is a nice dog though. I'm afraid I am getting attached."

Freddy examined me briefly.

"Look, Aunt Ida. Did you see he has a bobbed tail? I didn't notice that before. I wonder if he was born that way or if they bobbed it after he was born. I can't imagine someone bobbing a collie's tail. That's one of their best features. Maybe we should call you Bob. We have to call you something. What do you think, Bob? Or do you prefer Bobbie?" he said. I barked in agreement and offered my paw to cement the deal.

"Why, it seems as if he knows his name already. Maybe he really is a Bob," Uncle Bill said.

"You poor fellow. You must miss your master, don't you? And they must miss you too. If you were my dog, I know I would be looking everywhere for you. As much as I like you, I do hope your owners show up," Aunt Ida said.

For the time being, I felt at home. But I still missed my family, despite their faults. There had been only one other time where we had been separated. I did not take to that very well, either.

15

The Reo Café

$\mathcal{J}$UST WHEN I WAS SETTLING INTO MY NEW LIFE on the Abiqua farm, my world turned upside down. Frank bought a restaurant in town, and the family was moving there to operate it. That meant leaving the farm. What I didn't know, until the last minute, was that Frank had sold me to Mr. Peterson who was taking over the farm.

One day, I was on the front porch as Mr. Peterson counted out the cash into Frank's hands.

"That should do it, Tom. I know you'll take good care of Bobbie. I hate to leave him behind, but living in town is not the kind of life for a dog like him. He'd go crazy with nothing to do and no room to run," Frank said.

"Don't worry, Frank. He's in good hands. Bobbie will be just fine. You can come and visit him anytime you want," Mr. Peterson said.

I gave Frank one of my best pleading looks, but he wouldn't look me in the eye. Instead, he walked toward the automobile where the rest of the family was. Nova had been crying for the past few days, but until now, I didn't know why. She ran up to me and put her arms around me.

"I'll never forget you, Bobbie. I promise I'll come and visit you as often as I can. I love you my little Bobbin," she said. She then turned to leave.

This wasn't happening. I had to get in the automobile. They couldn't help but take me along if I were in the automobile. I climbed onto the running board and tried to get into the seat beside Leona and Nova.

"Bobbie, you stay here. Stay," Frank said in a stern voice. I hung my head down and my tail between my legs. "Don't give me that look. You know I hate that look."

Mr. Peterson took a rope and tied it around my neck.

"I won't have you following the car, Bobbie," he said as he tightened the knot.

Nova leaned out of the automobile. Her face was flushed, and her eyes were red from crying.

"Bye, Bobbie, be a good boy," she said through her tears. "You'll be sure to play ball with him won't you Mr. Peterson, and he should be brushed often. Otherwise, the burrs get stuck in his fur, and it's impossible to get them out. And don't let him dig for too many gophers. He loses teeth every time he does."

Mr. Peterson nodded his gray head. "I'll take good care of Bobbie. Don't you worry," he said.

Frank started the auto and drove off. Elizabeth stared straight ahead and looked very much as if she was trying not to cry. Even Leona's eyes were glistening as they drove away. Nova waved goodbye until they were out of sight.

I barked and strained at the awful rope around my neck.

"There, there, Bobbie. You'll be fine. I'll take good care of you. Hush now," Mr. Peterson said. He led me into the house and untied me. I ran to the window and then to the door. I barked, whined, and scratched to go out.

"Mattie, I think we better keep Bobbie in the house for a while, at least for a few days until he gets used to the new arrangement. I just paid good money for him, and I don't want him running off," he said shaking his head. "I've never seen a dog put up such a fuss."

For the next few days, they confined me to the house, except for when I was working the cows.

Eventually, I slipped off by myself and searched all the nearby farms for my family. Each day I widened my circle and went farther down the road. I learned that if I was gone too long Mr. Peterson was not pleased, and he gave me a whipping when I returned. I suppose he thought that would stop me—but it didn't.

One day, I wandered right into the center of Silverton. I trotted up and down the main streets looking for some sign of my family.

As I was about to cross Water Street and the bridge spanning Silver

Creek, I caught the wonderful smell of grilled meat wafting in the wind. Tempted by the possibility of a snack, I veered in the direction of the aroma. Intermingled with the food vapors, my nostrils detected another scent that was familiar.

As I walked past Mac's Place, Dickerson's Variety Store, and the bank, I came to a plain, clapboard building and large windows with gold lettering on them.

From the door, I could smell the wonderful, savory food. Sausages. Ham. Pancakes with marionberry syrup. Inside, people were sitting at tables covered in white cloths, silverware, and flowers. On one side was a long counter with wooden stools also filled with people. Several large ceiling fans quietly swirled near the ceiling, stirring the potted plants by the windows. A man in a white apron was going from table to table with a pitcher of water. He moved quickly across the diamond-patterned floor, stopped in the center of the restaurant, and spotted me by the door. He opened his mouth as if to say something when a woman behind the counter yelled out, "Mother, look who's here! It's Bobbie!"

I looked up and saw a woman in a blue dress with a white apron and a little white hat on her head. It was Leona!

"Mother, Nova, come here quickly," she called out.

Elizabeth came through a swinging door from the back of the room. She was wearing a long, white apron. I ran down the aisle between the tables and counter, and jumped up on her. Her eyes were wide with surprise.

"Bobbie, what are you doing here? Girls, he must have run off from the farm. Now, what are we going to do? Nova, take him out back and tie him up for now. When we're done with the breakfast rush we'll have to take him back," she said.

She shook her head and sighed, but I could see her force back a smile. Nova led me by the collar to the back room as a trail of giggles followed us out.

"Bobbie, you silly dog, how on earth did you find us? Bobbie-Bobbin! You were very bad to run away from home. Now we're going to have to make a special trip just to take you back. Mother isn't pleased. And you know what that means. You stay here and be a good boy," she said as she tied me up.

Later on that day, Frank drove me back to the farm and told Mr. Peterson the whole story.

"Well, Bobbie knows every farm and haystack between here and Silverton. All the neighbors say they have spotted him around their place.

It doesn't surprise me that he made it all the way to town," Mr. Peterson said.

"You might want to keep an eye on him for a while. Now that he knows the way, he might just be inclined to wander off again," Frank said.

"We certainly will," Mr. Peterson said taking the rope from Frank.

When Frank had disappeared in a cloud of dust down the road, Mr. Peterson whipped me again with the rope tied to my collar.

However, despite the whippings, I found a way to wander into town a few times a week. Soon, the regulars at the Reo knew me by name and I came and went as I pleased. I would spend a few days in town and then return to the farm, usually on Mondays.

Finally, one day, Frank drove out to the farm and had a long talk with Mr. Peterson.

"If I had known that Bobbie was going to get a beating every time he disobeyed, I would have thought twice before I sold him to you. Here, this is a fair offer for him. That's three times what you paid for him," Frank said.

"…Thirteen, fourteen, and fifteen. That'll do. I guess I can get another dog to do the same job. One that isn't going to run off," Mr. Peterson said giving me a hard look.

Afterward, Frank walked to his automobile, opened up the door, and stood with a big grin on his face.

"Well, Bobbie! What are you waiting for? Let's go," he said.

He then tooted his horn, as was his habit when he wanted me to come. I couldn't believe my ears. This could mean only one thing. I was going to be with my family at last.

16

The Great Escape

I LINGERED AROUND DES MOINES for a number of days mostly to check out the tourist camp, but there was still no sign of my family. One day, as it was nearing dusk, I headed toward Aunt Ida's house. I was thinking about the fresh meat that I was sure would be waiting for me, when I heard a vehicle coming up behind me on the road. It was a truck with a large cage on the back filled with barking dogs.

There were two men inside the cab of the truck. As they came around the curve, one of the men spotted me on the side of the road.

"Look it there, Fred. I think we got ourselves a straggler. He must be an escapee. I better pull over," the driver said.

I felt uneasy as the truck coasted to a stop along the side of the road. I picked up my pace, as the man on the passenger side stepped out. He walked slowly toward me.

"Hello there, fella. What are you doing all alone out here by your-self? You look lost. Come here, fella. Come on now. I won't hurt you," he said.

I avoided him like a porcupine and was ready to turn heels when he reached in his pocket, pulled out some pieces of dried liver, and tossed them in my direction. I eyed them suspiciously. He threw another piece just a bit closer to him. I hesitated, which was my undoing. While I pondered the dried meat lying in the dirt, the other man had come behind me and slipped a noose around my neck. I spun around, tossing my head back and forth. I pulled with all my strength, digging my feet into the dirt, but the noose only tightened around my neck. The man dragged me to the back of the truck.

"Come and help me here! He's a strong one. I can't handle him and the lock at the same time," he said.

The other man undid the lock, and when the doors opened, all the dogs inside went crazy, barking, and straining at the ropes tied to the sides of the truck. Their eyes were wild with panic.

The men lifted me into the truck and tied me to the side like all the others. Then they shut the doors, leaving us in the dark. I heard the engine come to life, and the truck started moving.

I knew this could lead to no good. The first thing I did was to chew through the rope to set myself free. Some of the other dogs got the same idea. Those that didn't catch on barked in frustration as the rest of us moved about. There was no way out, except through the back doors.

After awhile, the truck came to a stop. I heard other dogs barking off in the distance.

The men got out of the truck, unlocked the cage, and as the doors opened, I lunged up against them with all my strength. The doors flew open, slammed against the faces of the men, and they stumbled backward onto their rears. I leapt out of the truck and off into the night. I didn't look back but heard the wild scrambling of the other dogs as they followed my lead. I wasn't sure what direction I was going. I didn't care. I just wanted to get away from those men. Their curses trailed after me, as well as the mournful howl of the dogs who were left behind. There was no time for sympathy. It was every dog for himself.

When I came to a sharp curve in the road, I could see the lights of a vehicle rounding the corner. It took the curve too fast and veered in my direction. I tried to get out of the way, but I didn't have a chance. The next thing I remembered was flying across the ditch and everything going black.

17

The Vigil

OUT OF THE DARKNESS, I felt a fog creep over me. The ground became cold. Cold and damp as Toodles' grave. *I remember now. This is where they put Toodles. They put him in the cold ground.* After he hadn't eaten for several days, they took him away in the automobile, and when they came back, Elizabeth had him bundled up in his favorite blanket. Her face was red and puffy as she placed him on the ground behind the barn.

"At least the doctor was able to chloroform him. I'm not sure I could have watched him suffer anymore," she said.

He was so still. Not even a whisper of a breath. I tugged at his blanket. Nothing. I yanked, pawed, and barked. But he didn't move. What was wrong with him?

Nova put her arms around me.

"There, there, Bobbie, leave Toodles alone. He can't play anymore," she said.

It was then that I knew what was wrong. Toodles' heart, as well as his legs, had finally given out.

I stayed by Frank's side as he dug a hole behind the barn. He placed Toodles in the hole and shoveled the loose dirt on top of him. I jumped into the hole and frantically dug the dirt back out again.

"Bobbie, no! Stop that. Go lie down!" Frank said.

I did what he said, but every shovelful of dirt sent a shiver through me as Toodles disappeared from sight. When Frank placed a ring of stones around the hole, I inched my way on top of the soft earth and refused to move.

"Bobbie, come along now. We need to go in," Frank said. He grabbed me by the collar, but I gave out a wail and he let go.

"Bobbie, please come in out of the rain. You'll get sick...Oh, have it your way. I never saw a dog carry on so."

I stayed by Toodles' grave all through the night. At one point, the lights came on in the house, and Frank yelled at me from the back door.

"Bobbie, stop your hollering and come on in."

But I refused to budge. When I awoke in the morning, my fur was soaked from the overnight rain and caked with mud from the freshly-turned earth.

18

The Road to Recovery

*I*WAS COLD. COLD TO THE BONE. As I opened my eyes, the darkness gave way to gray. I was in some sort of ditch, and I couldn't move. I heard the crunching of footsteps on the gravel road. It was two young boys with book bags coming in my direction.

As I lifted my head, a sharp pain ripped through my spine, and I cried out.

"Geez, that dog's been hit. Poor fella. Hey, isn't that the stray that's been over at the Plumb's house?" one of them said.

"Yep, that's him all right. He's hurt bad. Why don't you run up there and see if anyone is home. I'll stay here with him," the other boy said.

"But we'll be late for school…" the first one said.

"Well, we can't just leave him here to suffer. Go on. I'll take the guff for it if we get in trouble."

The first boy ran down the road and awhile later Uncle Bill, Freddy, and the boy arrived in an automobile.

I cried out in pain as they tried to move me. Uncle Bill took a cloth strip and wrapped it around my muzzle.

"Don't want him lashing out at any of us," he said.

As he hoisted me onto a blanket, I strangled another cry as every muscle in my body went into a spasm of pain.

They each grabbed a corner of the blanket and hoisted me out of the ditch and into the automobile.

When we returned to the house, Aunt Ida directed them to the back room off the kitchen. They lowered me onto a pile of blankets spread on the floor.

"I've already called the vet. He's leaving right away. He lives just across town. Freddy, would you put some water on the stove to heat. We can fill up some hot-water bottles to warm him up. Bill, let's get him cleaned up. It's hard to tell how bad he's hurt with all this mud all over him. What do you suppose happened to him?" she said.

"My guess is he was hit by a car. He was lying just off the road. With all that fog last night…" Uncle Bill said.

Aunt Ida gently washed the mud from my fur and paws and by the time the veterinarian arrived, I was cleaned up. As he examined me, every prod felt like a sharp tooth in my spine. I wanted to crawl away and curl into a ball.

"Well, I don't think there are any broken bones. He has an old scar on his hip and above his eye, but those are old injuries. He's also missing a few front teeth, but there's no bleeding or other sign of injury to the mouth. Therefore, he must have lost them sometime before this. It looks as if his left hip took the worst of the blow. He's got some abrasions and swelling. He's going to be really sore for at least a few days. Try to keep him quiet and warm. These things take time. It could be a couple of weeks before he's himself again. I have something that'll sedate him for the next day or so. I'll come back later and check on him," he said.

Over the next week, Aunt Ida watched over me like a newborn, cleaning my wounds, and warming hot-water bottles. At night, before she went to bed, she warmed a saucer of milk for me and massaged my sore muscles.

However, despite Aunt Ida's nursing, I developed a bad cough. My head ached with fever, and my lungs became so heavy it felt as if someone was lying on top of me.

The veterinarian came out and looked me over again. He listened to my breathing through a tube that led to his ears.

"Sounds as if some fluid has settled in his lungs. I think he has pneumonia. He needs to move about. Even just a little bit, a few times a day," he said.

Thereafter, Aunt Ida, Uncle Bill, and Freddy took turns coaxing me to my feet and out-of-doors. After a few days, my lungs began to clear.

The sharp pain in my hip ebbed to a dull ache, and I finally could walk without my legs curling up beneath me.

After several weeks of recovery, I was able to walk normally if not a little bit slower than usual.

One afternoon, as I lay on the porch in the pale sunshine, I noticed the trees were nearly bare. Only a few, brittle leaves of the old oaks rattled in the wind, and I could smell a cold dampness in the air.

The next day, Aunt Ida was up at dawn and began preparations for a big meal. She placed a great bird in the oven, and the house filled with the wonderful smell of roasting meat.

Large platters and tureens adorned the dining room table, along with creamy-white candles and bowls of fruit and flowers.

Aunt Ida's sisters, Uncle Bill's brother, various cousins, and grand-nieces sat at the long table with the glistening china and glassware, as they ladled their plates with mounds of savory-smelling food.

My appetite had returned, and Aunt Ida rewarded me later with a plate of the bird's remains, just as Elizabeth used to do.

Everything about Aunt Ida's house reminded me of my family back home. The way they let me sit in the parlor in the evening; even how Freddy let me straddle his lap just as Frank would do.

However, despite the warmth of Aunt Ida's family, I became restless. Once again, the sun was setting in the west. I knew that is where I needed to be. And the time had come for me to leave.

I remained with the Plumbs through the night. At first light, when everyone was still asleep, I pushed open the door to the sleeping porch where I first met Freddy. I glanced to the cot where I first saw him sleeping. It seemed so long ago. I left quietly, but not without some heartfelt regret.

19

Cross the Wide Missouri

MY MUSCLES WERE STILL WEAK from my recuperation, so my pace was slow as I faced the cold prairie wind. My first day out, the sky remained clear. But by the next day dark, gray clouds appeared, carrying a river of rain with them. It rained cats and dogs and then Great Danes. The side of the road became slick, and my coat was caked with mud once again.

Because of my appearance, I was not exactly welcomed with open arms in the small towns and farmhouses across Iowa. I scrounged for food out of garbage cans and at restaurant back doors.

After a few days, I came to the town of Council Bluffs, overlooking the Missouri River. I recognized it immediately. I remembered Frank told a story about a couple of fellows named Lewis and Clark who had an important meeting with the Indians here.

The Missouri was churning with recent rain and was the color of brown gravy. "The Big Muddy" is what Frank said the Indians called it, and now I could see why.

I spotted the bridge that we had crossed on our way from Omaha to Council Bluffs. The "Askarben" bridge.

"That's Nebraska spelled backward," Frank had said.

Like the bridge over the Mississippi, the Askarben had toll guards stationed at the halfway point. I stayed close to the waterfront until darkness fell, and then I made my move.

At first, I did not see anyone in the bridge keeper's tower, even though there was a light shining through the small windows. A heavy rain began to fall and I thought, with luck, it would allow me to pass unnoticed. When I was within a few yards of the tower, a man in a dark hat and slicker poked his head out of the door and shined his lantern in my direction.

"Well, well, what do we have here? Can't tell for sure if it is some mangy, tramp dog or a coyote," he said to the other man inside the tower.

"Well, you better shoot it. You'd be doing the farmers a favor. Looks to me as if it could be a wild dog," the other man said poking his head out.

"Hand me the rifle, will ya," the man in the slicker said.

The man held the gun up and took aim. I was halfway across, and there was no place for me to hide.

I darted past them on the other side, zigzagging across the bridge. I heard gunshots and the ping of bullets meeting metal. Out of sheer panic, I leapt off the bridge into the inky water below. I floated through the air for what seemed like forever. The lights on the shore spun around as I splashed into the river. The freezing water soaked through my coat, and my body became heavy and numb. The strong current carried me under.

I saw faint lights on the shore and paddled toward them. Suddenly, a large, floating limb struck me on the side of the head. I choked on some water, and then I lost consciousness.

⚓

When I awoke, I was lying on the shore in a pile of debris. How I had gotten there, I don't know. The rain had stopped, and a dense fog had settled over the river. The lights on the shore were no longer visible, but I could hear the muffled sounds of train whistles, boat engines, and the river lapping against the wooden pilings. My head throbbed so badly it hurt to blink. I hobbled toward the road at the end of the bridge.

I came to some train tracks parallel to the road. They converged with other tracks near a large, brick building. I recognized this as the train station Frank and Elizabeth had driven by when leaving Omaha. A large engine was huffing and puffing in the station. Sleepy passengers gazing out on the gray morning filled the cars.

At the end of the platform, two men were loading luggage, crates, and large canvas bags onto one of the railroad cars.

As I approached, the taller of the two men called to his friend and pointed at me. "Look there, Mike, that dog's in pretty bad shape. Looks as if he went for a swim."

He jumped down off the railroad car and walked slowly toward me. My instinct was to run away, but he spoke softly and had a kind look.

"Come here, boy. Let me take a look at you," he said holding his hand out to me. I walked tentatively toward him. My head hurt so badly I could barely hold it up. The pain shot right through to my eyes, and everything became a blur. The man knelt down, and I walked up to him and offered my paw.

"Well, how do you do? What a clever boy. You poor fellow. You've been hurt. I bet you haven't had a decent meal in a long time. Mike, look at him. He's been on the road for some time. He must be lost," he said.

"He does look sort of dazed, Dave. You know how a bird looks when it flies into a window. Maybe he got hit or something," Mike said.

Dave examined my head and felt me all over.

"He's got a big old bump on the side of his head. Maybe a car hit him. Or maybe some mean son-of-a-gun gave him a wallop across the noggin. I wonder if someone tried to dump him in the river. Hey fella, this isn't the time of year to go swimming."

He walked over to the side of the brick building where he found an old pan, filled it with water, and offered it to me. Despite my dunk in the river, I was thirsty. The cool water soothed my burning fever.

"Seems a shame to just let this poor guy find his way on his own. There must be something we can do. It looks to me like he needs a nice, long rest. Hey, Mike, what do you say we set up a place for this guy to sleep inside the car? Hardly anyone but us comes back here anyway," Dave said.

"All right with me, but we need to keep him out of sight just in case anyone does go snooping," Mike replied.

They lifted me up into the car. Dave piled some burlap sacks on the floor and stacked some large boxes all around to create a little den for me. The minute I laid down on the pile of sacks, I fell into a deep sleep.

Later, I awoke to a rattling sound and realized the train was moving. Where were we going? I panicked. I looked for a way to escape, but the

The strong current carried me under.

large doors were now shut. Only a small, barred window allowed any light through. I climbed on top of the crates to look out and see where the train was heading. It took me awhile to get my bearings, as my head still throbbed and everything was blurry. The pale, gray clouds hung low to the ground, as curls of mist floated about. There was nothing but flat prairie, mile after mile. The only landmark I recognized was the Platte River that ran parallel to the tracks. Large flocks of migrating geese, herons, and ducks swarmed the marshy shorelines and sandbars of the broad, flat river.

I remembered my family had followed the Platte River when we came across, and that the railroad tracks followed the river. Maybe that meant the train was going in the right direction.

Eventually, I explored the boxes, wooden crates, trunks, suitcases, and assorted bags that filled the railroad car. The hours passed while I paced up and down the train car. The gray sky at the window turned to black and night set in. The train made a number of stops. I could hear the train whistle fill the night air, and the shouts of the conductors. I jumped on top of the crates and peeked out the window. I barked, but no one paid attention, and they left me alone.

The train rolled on into the night. Through the window, I could see the clearing night sky and the reflection of the moon as it skipped across the water. The blue light spilled out over the rolling, bare hills and flat prairie, and the clouds cast dancing shadows across the shimmering grasses.

The rhythm of the train was soothing, and I finally collapsed onto a pile of sacks and fell into a deep sleep. I dreamt of a more eventful trip across Nebraska with my family.

20
Nebraska

THE OVERLAND MADE GOOD TIME on the relatively flat gravel roads of Nebraska. Frank had been right in his predictions that we would be able to drive along with great ease, despite a speed limit of fifteen miles an hour, which he ignored most of the time.

The roads were still rough in spots, but generally we drove on graded gravel or pavement, wide and straight as far as the eye could see. Because of our speed, I was not able to jump off, but had to stay put for excruciatingly long periods. It was frustrating to see the arrogant prairie dogs taunt me as we passed. A cloud of dust was our constant companion as we made it swiftly across the flat terrain. At times, the wind was at our back, and a fine layer of grit covered us. Elizabeth donned her goggles and at times put a veil over her face to keep from breathing in the dust. Even Frank resorted to tying his handkerchief across his nose in order to breathe.

The landscape remained the same for miles and miles. One day in Nebraska was pretty much like the next. There were golden wheat and cornfields, and prairies dotted with coneflowers and goldenrod.

We passed through the towns of Kimball, Sidney, and Chappell situated on Lodgepole Creek that joined with the Platte River farther east.

Our first night in Nebraska we camped at a place called River's Bend outside of Kearney, which is midway across the state. Fifty cents a car included electric lights, a cooking range, showers, and telephone.

In the evening, Frank and Elizabeth sat in some chairs overlooking the river. As the sun set, a breeze kicked up bringing some welcome relief from the heat of the day.

"Well, Frank, we've made it more than halfway to Indiana. It still amazes me that we can cover as many miles in just a few days as it took the pioneers months to travel," Elizabeth said.

"And to think, Elizabeth, this road is the same route the Indians, the mountain men, the Mormons and even the buffalo used to take. That's why they built the railroad here. It's the shortest route to the West," Frank said.

"Can you imagine traveling in this heat through mile after mile of nothing but flat prairie in a covered wagon? I don't know if I could have done it," Elizabeth said.

"I guess, if it was up to us, the West would have remained untamed," Frank said.

The next day, the air was cooler, but by midmorning, it became hot and muggy again. Few trees offered any shade and the sun's heat seemed to magnify in this flat land. You could see heat waves rippling across the flat road for miles ahead. Soon Frank and Elizabeth were lamenting the more interesting, as well as cooler, atmosphere of the mountains in Wyoming.

"I don't know why people would want to live in such a barren land. There is nothing of interest to look at. Except maybe the river. How I miss our mountains. And I can't stand the heat. It's so oppressive," Elizabeth said.

"Well, Elizabeth, we have only about five hundred more miles to go," Frank said laughing. Elizabeth moaned as she squinted against the sun through her goggles.

By mid-afternoon, dark, purple clouds appeared on the horizon.

"It looks like it could rain soon, Elizabeth. That would be nice. A little rain will cool things off and help settle some of this dust," Frank said.

For the next couple of hours, the dark clouds skirted the horizon and slowly made their way overhead. A strong breeze kicked up little eddies of dust across the plains. Soon the clouds turned black, and their flat bottoms hovered close to the ground. Off in the distance, dark-blue streaks of rain poured from the clouds. Long before we felt the rain, we could smell it. Soon we were caught in what Frank called a "typical Midwest thunderstorm."

Across the horizon, jagged streaks of lightning struck the earth illuminating the entire sky, and the wind whipped up a flurry of dust and debris.

"I don't like the look of this," Frank said as he pulled off the road.

As we watched, the sky turned the color of pea soup as the storm clouds tumbled and churned overhead. Then, the wind died down and everything was very still.

Toward the horizon, a large, blue finger of a cloud came out of the mass of blackness and pointed toward the earth, stirring up dust as it snaked its way along the ground.

"Oh my goodness, Frank, is that a twister? Oh, dear, I hope it doesn't come this way. What should we do?" Elizabeth said as she gripped his arm.

"It still looks pretty far away, Elizabeth, and doesn't seem to be heading in this direction. I think we'll be all right, but I guess we should try to keep moving just in case that twister changes its mind," he said in a shaky voice.

I didn't like the look of that "twister" as they called it. I had never seen such a thing. I had never seen such a storm before. The air smelled funny, and the pressure made my ears hurt. I eyed the sky suspiciously and started to whine. I wanted to get away from there as soon as possible.

"What's the matter, Bobbie? That old twister got you nervous? I don't blame you, fella. It looks nasty. We should get moving and hope it goes in the opposite direction," said Frank.

He started up the car again and drove as fast as he could, despite the chuckholes and slick road. We kept an eye on the twister to see what path it was taking, and it still seemed to be far away.

"What should we do, Frank, if it catches up with us?" Elizabeth said.

"Well, usually, you're supposed to go into a root cellar or some such underground place. When caught out in the open like this, you should find a ditch or gully to lie down in. So keep your eye out for some sort of natural low point. Even an irrigation ditch would do," he said.

The twister curled its way in our direction a few times but then veered off again. We seemed to be moving in opposite directions, which was a relief to all of us.

After what seemed like a very long time, the blue-black finger faded back into the clouds.

"Well, that is something I could go a lifetime and be glad not to see again," Elizabeth said letting out a long sigh. "Oh, dear, my heart won't stop racing."

"I don't think we were in any real danger, Elizabeth, but I'm glad it's over as well. What about you, Bobbie? Did that ole twister scare you?" he called to me in the back seat.

I lifted my head up from the seat where I had been crouching and gave him a few sharp barks.

Soon the heavy rain let up, the clouds parted, and the sun streaked through. A peculiar odor filled the air.

"Frank, does it smell like rotten eggs to you? I remember now how it always smells like that after a big storm," Elizabeth said.

"That's caused by the electricity in the lightening, I believe. I think it's sulfur. Reminds me of that mineral water we pumped from the well outside of Point of Rocks, Wyoming," Frank said.

"Well, at least the worst is over. It's so cool and fresh now. I hope that was the last twister we see this trip. Amazing how such a plain, barren land can look so beautiful after such an experience. Why, look, Frank, there is even a rainbow. How lovely! Frank, don't you think you should slow down just a little. The road is awfully slick," she said as she grabbed his arm.

"Some Nebraska gumbo isn't a problem for me," he said.

Just as he said this, the Overland skidded a few feet across the road. Frank turned red in the face and quickly reduced his speed.

Elizabeth laughed and said, "We make it through a twister, but end up in a ditch after all."

21

North Platte

OVER THE CYCLE OF A FEW DAYS I woke up, drank, and ate what was left for me in some bowls, looked out the small window of the train, and then I fell back to sleep again. The rest did me good. The swelling on my head went down, and I felt like my old self once again.

One morning I awoke to the sound of the large, wooden doors sliding open and to sunlight streaming in. It was Mike and Dave, the two men who had put me in there.

"Look here. The food we left is gone again. He must be feeling better. Where is he?" Mike said.

"He's gotta be here somewhere. Here boy!" Dave said. He gave a short whistle. I saw he had a length of rope in his hand and knew enough to avoid him at all cost.

As they moved away from the door, I slipped out from behind the boxes, and when the way was clear, I bolted for the door.

"There he is, grab him," Mike said as he tripped over some mailbags and fell to his face. Dave was a little faster and made a leaping lunge for me, but missed and landed on top of Mike.

As I jumped from the train, I could hear them squabbling and scrambling to their feet. Without looking back, I ran down the long, wooden platform, past all the people, and past the brick train depot.

Something was familiar about the place—the sign above the entrance, the smells coming from the dining room. This was the same depot where Frank and Elizabeth had eaten lunch on our trip east.

I had no time to dwell on this new discovery and hurried down the street, and away from the two men. After a mad dash down several alleyways, I lost all sight of them.

At the west entrance to town, I recognized the iron archway with the portrait of a man with a large, white hat, and white mustache and beard.

"North Platte. The home of Buffalo Bill Cody," Frank had said.

I walked beneath the archway and into the main part of town. Despite the earliness of the hour, there were a number of people about. I came to a small café that was bustling with customers.

The sound of tinkling glasses and silverware, as well as the familiar smells of bacon, eggs, and flapjacks made me homesick for the Reo Café, and for my family. I was also hungry. I couldn't remember a time when I wasn't hungry.

There were several automobiles parked out front of the café. One of them was packed with suitcases and other equipment. Its sides were splattered in mud and smelled of the road.

I lurked around the front door of the café looking for a soft touch. I didn't have long to wait. Soon, a man and woman with two young boys came out. They were bundled up against the cold of the morning and moved quickly toward the auto with all the boxes and trappings attached. They were laughing and seemed to be in a good mood. I waited as they got into their vehicle to see what direction they were going. When it was clear they were heading west, I ran alongside and barked to get their attention.

The woman looked down at me running alongside the wheels.

"Richard, I think you better stop. That dog is following us. Maybe he's lost," she said.

The man stopped the auto, and I jumped onto the running board.

"Dad, he wants to get in. He must be lost. See the frayed rope around his neck? Maybe he ran away," one of the boys said.

The father, a large, round man with a wide-brimmed hat on his head, gave me a once over.

Without blinking an eye, he said in a booming voice, "What the hey, bring the fellow along. He looks a little worse for wear. Could only be doing him a favor. Even if he does have an owner around here, they obviously don't take very good care of him. Let the fellow sit in the back out of the wind."

As soon as I was safely in the back seat, the man continued out of town. The road followed the river and the railroad tracks, and was the same route I remembered taking with my family.

Feeling confident things were under control, I took a nap on the seat in between the two young boys. When I woke up, we were still following the river as well as the railroad tracks. As we drove on into early evening the moon rose, illuminating the snow-capped mountains on the horizon.

Richard was in good spirits and told jokes that made the others groan. They all laughed and sang songs as we drove along. The time passed quickly. Getting a ride was not a bad idea, especially through the mountains. At this rate, I'd be home before I knew it.

We came to a large city perched on the slopes approaching the mountains. However, something was wrong. I did not know this place. I knew my family and I had not come this way. The mountain range was not as I remembered.

What I did not know at the time was that Richard had taken the road following the South Platte River and not the North Platte as my family had done coming east.

As we pulled into town, Richard said, "I don't know about you but I'm starving. Let's find out what kind of steaks Denver has to offer."

When they spotted a diner alongside the road, Richard pulled over and they all went inside, leaving me to wait in the car.

While they were gone, I jumped out the window and headed down the darkened streets.

I needed to find the right road toward home. First, I needed to find some food. I came to a residential district and looked for garbage cans, or for food left out for other pets. As I was checking the front porch of one house, I heard the sound of a horn and saw a car pulling up the gravel driveway.

"Oh, my goodness, where did that dog come from?" a woman in the front seat said.

"He must be a stray. Look how scruffy and skinny he is. He must have come a long way," the man next to her said. "Maybe he followed a cart in from the country. I don't think I have ever seen him around here before. Have you? He must be hungry, that's why he's here. What a little beggar."

I ran to them as they were getting out of their car, and greeted them with a few well-timed whimpers and pleading looks.

"Poor thing. Why don't you kids take him to the back porch and I'll find him something to eat," the woman said.

The three children led me to the back of the house, and soon the mother came out with a pan of food. I sat politely and offered a paw for her to shake.

"What a gentleman you are. How do you do. Can you speak as well?" she asked me. I knew what "speak" meant, and I gave her a sharp bark that made her jump.

"Well, aren't you a clever fellow," she said as she put the food down for me.

I ate the food quickly and gave her a wag of the tail as my way of appreciation.

"Mommy, look at his stubby tail," the little boy pointed out.

"They call that a bobtail, Christopher," she said. "Are you a little bobtail dog? Do they call you Bobbie?" she asked me.

When she said my name, I gave another bark and an even bigger wag of my tail.

"So you are a Bobbie. That was easy enough. Such a fine Bobbie you are. You must have had good owners to be so polite and well behaved. You look like you are a long way from home though," she said.

"He looks worn out, and his coat is all matted and full of burrs. It does look like he's been on the road for some time. He feels strong, even if he is skinny, so he must be getting some food," the father said as he felt up and down my body.

"What are we going to do with him, Dad," Christopher said.

"Well, for tonight, he can sleep in the basement, and then we will have to call around and see if anyone is missing a dog. I doubt he's from around here. Possibly from one of the ranches out of town. He looks like a good herding dog. I wonder what on earth would have brought him into town. He must have gotten lost from his owner. We'll call the Denver police tomorrow. There's nothing that can be done about it now," he said.

"He's so cute, Daddy. Doesn't he look like our Wonder?" one of the little girls said as she stroked my chest.

"Now that you mention it, he does look a bit like Wonder," the father said.

"Yes, he does. However, Wonder was so spoiled; he wouldn't do anything that didn't suit him. This fellow is much better behaved, and he'd be a good-looking dog if he were cleaned up. Maybe after dinner we can take care of that. In the meantime, I want all of you to wash up for supper. We have company coming, remember," Carrie said.

Later on, guests arrived, and along with the family made a big fuss over me. After dinner, they all gathered in the front room by the fireplace. Carrie gave permission for me to come into the front room after I had a thorough brushing.

I sat on the floor in front of the fireplace with the three children around me. They took turns stroking my head and chest. Every now and then, the fire would flare up and crackle as the wind made little eddies through the chimney.

I could barely keep my eyes open and soon dozed off. Later, the children led me to a room downstairs where they allowed me to spend the night. With the sound of the wind rattling about the house, I was grateful for a place out of the storm.

In the morning, Carrie greeted me in her robe and slippers with a long braid that fell over one shoulder. As she moved about the kitchen preparing the family's breakfast, she also prepared a dish of food for me. I ate it quickly and then scratched at the kitchen door to be let out.

"Why don't you let the dog out, Christopher? He probably needs to do his business. What a good dog to let us know," Carrie said.

As Christopher opened the door, a gust of wind hit him with such force, he had a hard time standing upright. I was tempted to retreat back into the warmth of the kitchen.

Christopher let me out and closed the door as quickly as he could behind me. As I stood on the front lawn, I noticed Carrie peering through the window with a look of confusion, and then sadness, on her face. I think she understood that I wasn't going to stay.

Therefore, I left the Abbee family and found myself, once again, alone in the world.

22

Winter in the West

I HEADED TOWARD THE CENTER OF DENVER. I had to find the road that would lead me back to the highway my family had come across on. The streets bustled with autos and trucks carrying people and goods around town. Because of the traffic, it was hard to make my way. I had become wary of trucks, ever since my accident in Des Moines, but I finally reached the edge of town.

Once leaving Denver, I headed north. I just knew that was the direction to get back on track. A cold, damp wind blew down from the snow-capped mountains to the west, and I could feel it in my bones.

After a number of days, I came to a smaller city that I recognized as being the one we had come through going east. Cheyenne. Many of the buildings, including the Capitol dome and the clock tower of the railroad station, were familiar. The mountains in the distance were also as I remembered. I passed by the same yellow-brick hotel where Frank and Elizabeth had stayed after the long trip through the mountains. They called it "the Plains." I remembered how Elizabeth had snuck me up to the room, while Frank distracted the clerk with questions about road conditions. That had been my first and only stay at a hotel.

A raw, biting wind whipped a fine dusting of snow across the streets of Cheyenne as I passed through. Other than scrounging for a meal, I didn't stick around long but pressed on toward the mountains ahead of me. As I climbed higher and farther away from civilization, the lights of Cheyenne faded behind me, as did the hope for any more easy meals.

The wind was a bitter companion and drove the snow so hard I couldn't see in front of me more than a few feet. I had never seen such a storm before. In my short life, it had snowed only once on our farm in Silverton, and then it only lasted for one day. Already, the snow covered everything in sight. Only the fence posts or electrical wires hinted as to where the road might be. I hardly knew where I was going or where I came from in the wide expanse of nothingness. I merely pressed onward in blind faith that I was going in the right direction. As night came, the storm raged on. I struggled through chest-deep drifts of snow until I was too exhausted to continue. I finally collapsed in my tracks.

As I lay there, with the wind blowing around me, my mind and body became numb, and I drifted off to sleep. I began to dream. I dreamt of a warm, summer day wading with Nova in the Abiqua, and of lying in the sun by the plum orchard. I dreamt of chasing chickens while my old friend Toodles watched.

Then I was with Elizabeth in the kitchen of the Reo as she was preparing for the rush of the lunch crowd. Through the door, I could see Billy Gable flirting with Leona.

"Give me some of that Buttercup ice cream, Leona," Billy said.

"What flavor, Mr. Gable?" Leona said.

"What's your favorite, Leona?" he said with a wide smile.

"Strawberry," she said blushing, while Clifton scowled from the end of the counter.

"Then strawberry it is," Billy Gable said with a wink.

Later, I was in the parlor, as Frank and Elizabeth poured over books and maps and planned their tour to Indiana. I was no longer cold and alone but among those I loved. I fell into a warm, deep sleep.

How long I was asleep, I don't know. When I awoke, I was stunned to find out that not only was I warm, but I was very much alive. I realized then I was buried in snow and that it had protected me from the biting wind. I stood up and shook off the mantle of snow. As I did, a world of blinding brightness was revealed to me.

As I tried to get my bearings, I spotted a pyramid-shaped object standing alone against the horizon. Something about it was familiar. I then recognized it as the same stone pyramid we had driven by coming east. "The Ames Monument" Frank had called it. The one erected in honor of Oliver and Oakes Ames, some important men who helped build the railroad. Frank had gone on and on about the importance of the railroad and the "taming of the West" as he called it. I slept through most of his lecture, but I remembered the monument. Frank had called this plateau "Sherman's Hill," and it was the highest point along the Lincoln Highway.

There was a small tavern at the top, but it looked abandoned. I scoured the outside for some traces of food, but I didn't find any.

The railroad tracks were nearby, and I used them to guide me in the right direction. I trudged westward through mile after mile of deep snow in the open rangeland. In the clear air, I could see the mountains Frank had called "Elk Mountain and Pike's Peak." The Medicine Bow range was to the west.

Farther west, I spotted another familiar landmark. Next to the road, in a small, fenced-off area, was a small, lone tree growing out of a rock. Frank had called it the "Tree in the Rock." It was the only tree for miles around. I remembered Elizabeth had bought something called a post-card at the hotel in Cheyenne that had a picture of the little tree on it. It must have been a very important tree.

I had not eaten since I left Cheyenne, and I was getting weak from hunger. Eventually, I found the tracks of a rabbit in the new snow. I tried tracking it, but it was not easy as the deep snow slowed me down. I was not without some skill. Hunting was something I had learned how to do back in Silverton with our neighbor's dog, Pilot.

23
Pilot

I HAD FIRST SPOTTED PILOT watching me silently from the shadows of the fir trees above our farm. He took me by surprise, and I prepared to slink off. Part wolf and black as coal, he was almost twice my size. However, he did not make any threatening gestures, so I stood my ground. We eyed each other for a moment, and then he calmly walked toward me. As he approached, I crouched down and flicked my tongue at his muzzle to let him know I meant no challenge. Pilot gave me a good sniffing and then, without any additional formalities, invited me to play by bowing down in front of me. I jumped up and met him eye to eye. He came alongside of me and placed his head on the back of my neck. I pivoted around, jumped up, and placed both my front paws on his back. He quickly maneuvered out from beneath me, ran a few paces away, and then did another turn-about-face and challenged me again.

I charged at him, leaping, and nipping at his face, legs, and hindquarters. I growled and snarled. Pilot remained silent and easily dodged my most determined thrusts. He zigzagged and then turned to face me again. Pilot countered each move of mine, until he silently and effortlessly pinned me on my back and placed his huge jaws around my throat. He held me there for a few moments and then let me up.

Pilot's play was not the play of my childhood, nor was it the play I shared with Toodles. Despite his smile and easy-going manner, I knew he was powerful, and that the wolf in him was just below the surface.

It became a habit for us to wander together through the hills around his home. He knew the backwoods as well as I knew our farm. It was on these excursions that I learned about the art of hunting and about Pilot's true nature.

One time, as we were crossing a clearing, he spotted a young cottontail in a raspberry patch. Pilot froze in his tracks. An intense, fixed gaze replaced his large, easy-going grin. He crouched low to the ground and became silent.

I didn't understand why he did not just chase it, as the most fun was in the chasing. I decided he was wasting time, so I charged across the clearing and chased the rabbit into the heavy undergrowth of vines.

When I lost track of the rabbit, I returned to where Pilot was. He turned on me with a snarl and pinned me to the ground. It was his way of telling me I had done something wrong. I decided that I would follow his lead.

We walked silently for a while until we spotted another young rabbit chewing on the leaves of the raspberry vines. I watched as Pilot quietly approached the unwary animal. He lowered his head and body until his belly almost touched the ground as he slowly crawled closer. The rabbit was oblivious to everything but the tender, new shoots. When Pilot was within a couple of yards of the rabbit, he sprang with full force upon his prey. The rabbit spotted him too late. He took off, but Pilot was on his backside before he left the ground. There was a piercing squeal that I would not have thought possible from such a small animal. A quick shake of the neck silenced him, and he went limp.

Up until then, I had never seen anything die, except for a few not-very-bright chickens whose heads were caught beneath an axe, and some gophers I had killed. Frank had taught me not to harm any of the animals on the farm. But watching Pilot take down that rabbit was something I would never forget.

24

Survival of the Fittest

I STRUGGLED THROUGH THE SNOW and rough country of the high plains of western Wyoming. There were many miles between towns and any sign of human habitation. I relied on whatever small rodents and rabbits I could kill to keep me alive.

One day I was listening to the stirrings of a mouse beneath the snow, ready to pounce, when I spotted a large pack of wolves—about seven strong—chasing a young antelope through the snow. The chase went on for some time before the antelope finally tired and floundered in the snow. The wolves circled the animal until it collapsed, and then they moved in for the kill. As the wolves tore at his back and throat, the animal lifted his head and gave out a long wail that echoed across the barren landscape and then fell silent.

The wolves ripped into the soft underbelly, and a plume of steam rose as the warm blood melted into the white snow. My mouth watered for some of the fresh meat. But I knew better than to approach the wolves while they were still gorging. I waited until even the smallest of the pack had its fill and wandered off.

When everything was quiet, I slipped down to where the remains were. The wolves' scent hovered around the carcass, but my hunger was greater than any fear I had of them.

By the time I reached the dead animal, several ravens had gathered and were pecking at the carcass. I tore at the remaining pieces of flesh. However, I soon discovered I was not alone. Several coyotes had gathered as well. They eyed me suspiciously, but their hunger overtook their fear and they closed in on the dead antelope.

As the scavengers crowded around, an old male wolf appeared out of the woods and watched us quietly from a distance. As he approached, I noticed that he was skin and bones and that he had a limp in his right foreleg. I was prepared to run off, but he made no threats toward the coyotes or me. He meekly approached the carcass and attempted to glean some of the meal for himself. I figured he was not part of the other pack of wolves but much like me—on his own. By the looks of him, this would be his last winter.

For a while, the only sounds heard were the cackling of the crows and the grinding of teeth on bones and sinew.

After awhile, a large female wolf returned and scattered us away from the remains. I ran off as fast as I could through the deep snow. The coyotes and the old wolf divided her attention, so I was able to elude her. The old wolf was not so lucky. I heard his cries of pain as I made my escape through the woods.

For days, I struggled through the snow west of Cheyenne. After Sherman's Hill, the plateau descended into a plain area rimmed by mountains.

I came to the town of Laramie just at dusk when the city lights were coming on. The wind had died down and everything was quiet.

I scoured the alleyways for something to eat. I found the remains of a frozen ham bone which I ate without chewing. I was to regret this, as it must have been spoiled and it only came up again. I was too tired to look for more food. Every muscle in my body ached from straining through the deep drifts of snow. I found a place to sleep next to a grate venting steam. Here, I settled in for some rest. I dreamt of the steak pieces that Frank had shared with me from his dinner at a restaurant here in town.

"That was the biggest steak I've ever ordered, Elizabeth. It must have been the size of Rhode Island," he said.

During the night, the sound of church bells and footsteps woke me. I crawled out of the window-well where I had been sleeping and investigated.

Several small groups of people were walking toward a church at the end of the street. I followed quietly behind to see what was going on. Besides, wherever people were, food was usually nearby.

The church doors were open, and music and light spilled out onto the street. In front of the church was a small, wooden structure filled with hay and statues of people kneeling around a little baby. This seemed like a good place to spend the rest of the night, so I snuck inside the shed and burrowed into the hay behind a life-sized statue of a donkey. Here I slept soundly, protected from the cold, and with the sound of music and singing floating on the night air.

Early the next morning, I awoke and found a large piece of nearly-frozen cake with fruits and nuts in it laid carefully next to me. I gobbled it up quickly. Outside the entrance to the church, I found the soggy remains of cookies and more cake.

The cake tasted much like some Elizabeth served on a night last winter. I remembered the family allowed me into the parlor. After dinner, they sat together around the fireplace listening to music on the radio. Everyone slipped pieces of cake to me when Elizabeth wasn't looking, even Leona.

My stomach still churned from the bad ham bone from the night before, but food was food.

I wandered the empty streets sniffing for something more substantial, but I did not stay long and continued west out of town. When Laramie was some distance behind me, I once again heard the sound of bells from several churches ringing through the cold air across the valley.

For days, I continued west through the towns of Medicine Bow, Carbon, and Rawlins, lingering only long enough to search for food. Past Creston Station, I crossed the Great Divide. The "backbone" of the continent is what Frank called it. I remembered how we had spent the day gradually climbing higher and higher. When we reached the Divide, we were hardly aware of it until Frank spotted a sign on the side of the road marking the spot. Frank and Elizabeth stopped here and had a leisurely lunch of sandwiches that they shared with me.

"This was where all the rivers east of the mountains flow to the east and all the rivers west flow to the Pacific Ocean. It's like sitting on top of the world, isn't it Elizabeth?" Frank had said in his professor voice.

"I guess I'll have to take your word for it Frank. It just doesn't seem like we are that high. If it weren't for the low clouds or those mountain peaks in the distance, I would think we were on just another plain. It's so flat around here," Elizabeth said.

Over the next weeks, I traveled through this lonely world, going for days without food because of lack of game. The prairie dogs and jackrabbits that had been plentiful during the summer were now as scarce as sunshine. Sometimes, I came across the mangled body of a rabbit in a trap or snare and made an easy meal of the remains. Once, along a frozen riverbed, I found the remains of a dead fish that I ate bones and all.

The nights were the worst. I had little protection from the ever-present wind or from other predators. Sometimes, my only shelter was under a ledge of rocks or a tunnel into the snow. As I lay there in the darkness, I heard the sound of the wind mingle with the howls of coyotes and wolves. Their cries echoed my own loneliness, and I joined the chorus of voices that filled the cold night air.

When day broke, I continued on my way. The road was barely visible beneath the layer of snow; but by observing the direction of the sun, as well as the placement of the telegraph poles next to the railroad tracks, I was able to guide myself in the right direction. In many stretches, there were double rows of stone fences erected along the highway to keep the snow from drifting across the road and railroad tracks, or to keep cattle contained. I used these to guide me as well.

A crust had formed across the surface of the snow and cut into the pads of my paws. Each step was like walking on broken glass. Eventually, a trail of bloody paw prints followed in my wake.

As I had remembered, the landscape became more barren as I approached the area Frank had called the "Red Desert." There were large expanses of sand dunes and sagebrush. Massive red rocks Frank called "hoodoos" stood out starkly against the white snow. From a distance, I spotted what looked like a large lake, but when I came nearer, I found nothing but flat, cracked earth with a whitish coating over the top. Water was scarce, and I went miles without water. I found a small spring near the surface of the soil, but I had to break through a thin coating of ice in order to drink.

Among the ranges of sagebrush, I spotted herds of wild horses scavenging for food. They were the only other sign of life in the area.

Beyond the Red Desert, were the ash-colored gorges of Point of Rocks where the sandstone bluffs formed fantastic shapes that loomed over the road. I remembered that Elizabeth had read aloud from the *Official Lincoln Highway Guidebook* that gave the rocks names such as Sancho's Bower, Hermit's Grotto, and the Cave of the Fairies. I rested in one of the caves before moving on. Nearby were a number of mineral springs that provided me with some much-needed water. It smelled funny, but I wasn't about to complain.

The Overland had mired in the soft sand near here. I remembered how Elizabeth had to take the steering wheel, while Frank wedged wooden planks and clumps of sagebrush under the tires to get us out. I remembered the look of triumph on Frank's face. However, we only went a few more miles when a rock punctured one of the tires, and he had to stop and repair it.

The next town I came to was Rock Springs, which I recognized by the metal archway at the entrance to town.

"Rock Springs Coal," is what Frank had said when he read the sign. He then told a story about how some of the buildings in town had been built over old coal mines, and that some of them had sunk into the ground when the mines collapsed.

I didn't see any buildings sunk in the ground, but I did find a number of cafés with garbage cans out back.

I gorged on soup bones and old dumplings before I continued west. Beyond that was the town of Green River. Even from miles away, I recognized the great red and brown monolith called Castle Rock, which hovered over the town. I remembered that we had camped beneath its shadow next to the river. I remembered the sound of train whistles echoing off the rocky cliffs.

As usual, I stayed only long enough to prowl around the train yards looking for food. I feasted on chicken skins and marrowbones. I was reluctant to leave another easy source of food, but I continued on, following the road through gorges of similar red-and-yellow-colored rock until I came to the town of Granger.

Here, I recognized the sand-colored building of the Overland station that Frank had pointed out. It was at this junction that we had changed highways. I found where the two roads met, and I left the Lincoln Highway and headed in a north-westerly direction on the Old Oregon Trail Highway. I remembered how Frank had gone into one of his long speeches about pioneers in covered wagons and the Oregon Trail, when I fell asleep. Now, I wished I had paid more attention.

I followed a winding, narrow pass through the mountains and the towns of Montpelier, Soda Springs, and Lava Hot Springs of Idaho.

During the summer, these places had been swarming with tourists, but now they were nearly deserted.

Once over these mountains, I came to a large, flat area rimmed by other mountain ranges and to the town of Massacre Rocks. I recognized the gas station and a soda fountain where Elizabeth had bought ice cream which she shared with me in a small paper cup, while Frank gave one of his lectures about a fight between the settlers and Indians at this place.

At the edge of the desert plain, and not too far from the Snake River, was the town of Pocatello. Beyond that was American Falls, where men had been building something Frank called a "dam" which he said would make the falls disappear and let the farmers irrigate their crops.

"Can't see how irrigation could help. Only crops that would grow around here are potatoes or sugar beets, and maybe onions. Our Willamette Valley seems like the Garden of Eden compared to this country," he said.

I followed the river until I reached the thunderous Shoshone Falls, which I remembered from our trip east. "The Niagara of the West" is what Frank had called it. During the summer, the mist from the falls cooled us down and was a refreshing stopover from the heat of the desert. Now, the great plumes of spray that rose from the chasm below froze on the rocky buttes overhanging the river.

I remembered how Frank tried to get some close-up pictures of the falls by climbing over the slippery rocks to get a better view.

He stood on the edge of the rocks, teetered, and waved his arms about, pretending to fall. Elizabeth stood by the car with her hands over her eyes.

"Frank, stop fooling around and get back to the car. You're making me nervous," Elizabeth yelled over the noise of the falls. She shook her head in disgust. "For a grown man, Frank, you have absolutely no sense sometimes."

I could still hear her voice even in the great rush of water. I continued on.

I passed a number of other familiar sights near the river including a great rock that stood on a small point like a question mark. Here, Frank took a snapshot of Elizabeth pretending to hold the rock up just as all the other tourists did.

Beyond that was a stretch of the river where numerous springs poured out of the limestone cliffs. Frank had called the place "Thousands Springs."

"This is where the Lost River re-emerges from the desert floor and drains into the Snake River," Frank had said.

I followed the road as it veered away from the river and through the desert that was lightly covered in snow. My feet became swollen from walking across rocks, and from the ice crystals that lodged between the pads of my feet. I was barely aware of the pain until I stopped moving.

Eventually, the highway led me to Boise, where I rested for several days and searched for food.

After Boise, I came to the Snake River again near the Idaho and Oregon border. Outside of Weiser, I passed the campsite where we had stayed. I crossed the river by means of the same steel bridge I had come across with my family.

Once I reached the other side and the river was behind me, I had a renewed sense of hope. Despite my aching body and sore feet, I knew home was that much closer.

In the distance, I could see the ridges of the Blue Mountains, which I knew I would have to cross as well. But once I did, I would have made it through the worst of it.

When I came to Baker City, I begged for food outside the kitchen door of one of the large hotels. Some crates in an alleyway were the only shelter I had through the night.

On the outskirts of the town, I recognized the ruts made by the wagons of the pioneers on their way to the Willamette Valley. Frank had pointed these out to Elizabeth. I continued across the high desert plains outside of Baker City, crossing the Powder and Grande Ronde rivers, and eventually reached the town of La Grande on the edge of the Blue Mountains. I rested there for a short while and scrounged a few meals before continuing.

As I was making my way through the mountain pass, I faced another winter storm. Rather than fighting my way through the blinding winds, I found shelter in the hollow of a tree. I spent part of a day and night curled into a ball against the cold.

In the morning, the powdery layer of snow revealed fresh rabbit tracks. I followed the trail, hoping for a meal of fresh meat. All of a sudden, I got a strong whiff of an unknown animal mingled in with the rabbit's scent. It lingered in the air like a vapor. My hair prickled at the strangeness of it. I wondered if this animal was near, but other than the odor, I didn't see anything. Farther on, I spotted the deep tracks of a large creature intermingled with the rabbit's tracks. Even though crazy with hunger, I stopped tracking the rabbit and looked for other game.

Farther on, I found another rabbit's trail that I followed into a dark, narrow canyon. The sharp rock ledges towered over me cutting me off from the rest of the world. It was unusually quiet. Then, suddenly, I heard a deep growl, and crouching on the ledge above me was a large cat unlike any I had ever seen. I froze in my tracks, unsure of what to do. Now the hunter had become the hunted. I knew I did not have a chance against such a strong animal.

He crouched, ready to pounce at any moment. As I braced myself for the worst, I suddenly heard the baying of hounds echoing off the canyon walls.

The cat's ears perked forward, and he looked in the direction of the noise. He growled and hissed. His hot breath became a cloud in the cold air. He broke from his crouching position and took off. When he was out of sight, I barked furiously more out of relief than threat. The hackles on my back remained stiff long after he disappeared from view.

...on the ledge above me was a large cat unlike any I had ever seen...

The baying of the hounds drew closer. I wasn't sure what to make of the situation, so I made myself scarce. As I slunk out of sight, I saw three hounds approach the spot where I had last seen the cat. With their noses to the ground, they circled frantically. I think they must have picked up my scent, but that only confused them for a moment. When they picked up the trail of the cat, they called the alarm and took after it. Clouds of sparkling, fresh snow scattered in all directions. I followed them from a distance and from the cover of a stand of trees.

As the sound of the dogs' barking became more urgent, I heard men shouting from farther down the canyon. The hounds came to the base of a large pine. Crouched on a branch above the ground was the snarling, hissing cat.

The men approached with their rifles ready, shouting to each other and at the dogs. Stealth was not their method of operation. I thought back to Pilot and how silently he hunted his prey. These men and their dogs did not seem to know what they were doing. By now, anything worth eating was long gone.

I heard the sharp crack of rifle shots bouncing off the canyon walls. The cat fell from the tree with a dull thud, and I felt the ground shake.

Jubilant cries broke the silence as the men ran toward the lifeless cat. As they gathered around, the man that shot him held the huge cat's head up in triumph as they all patted him on his back.

Once things quieted down, I thought of approaching the men. People usually meant food. I was still some distance from them as I came out of a stand of pine trees. One of the men spotted me, lifted his rifle, and took a couple of shots in my direction. I didn't know why, and I wasn't about to stick around to find out. I heard them shout as I disappeared, but they and their dogs did not trail after me.

Eventually, I made it through the Blue Mountains and came onto a great plain Frank had called the "Umatilla Plateau."

The next town I came to was Pendleton. At a remote ranch outside of town, I rested and found food. I continued through miles of flat range land with only the occasional herd of cattle or sheep for company.

Then one day, as I came to the top of a long hill, a great gust of wind hit me square in the muzzle, carrying the smell of water with it. Off in the distance, I spotted the Columbia River flanked by barren, brown hills. What a wonderful sight it was. I knew I could follow the river toward home.

The wind howled through the gorge, carrying with it a torrent of rain and sleet. It wasn't long before a thick coating of ice covered the road and trees. The pads of my feet became raw from walking through the frozen crust that covered everything. At one point, I stopped to rest for only a short time and my feet froze to the road. As I struggled to pull free, the ice tore at the raw patches on my pads and they started to bleed. Throughout the night, the wind blew with a vengeance. The river funneled the blast of air against the stony cliffs on each side. I heard the ice-coated limbs clicking and clacking above and the loud crack of trees crashing to the ground. I eventually found shelter in a tunnel that bored through the side of the mountain. Here I rested until daylight.

The next day, the wind continued to blow bringing with it more ice and rain. At the town of The Dalles, where the Deschutes River meets the Columbia, I found a family that sheltered me for the night. But, despite the storm, I left first thing the next day.

I followed the Columbia River through the gorge, past frozen waterfalls and large monoliths of stone that Frank had called "Cleopatra's Needle" and "Castle Rock." As I headed west, the sparse cliffs that were dotted with pine and juniper gave way to forests of Douglas fir and hemlock.

For days, I followed the river until it led me to the outskirts of the city of Portland, where I found the road that led away from the river and through the residential district. When darkness fell and I couldn't go any farther, I crawled onto the back porch of an old house and collapsed, unable to move. A small white-haired woman came to the door.

"Oh my…Joseph and Mary, what do we have here…?"

I was barely conscious as she slid me onto a blanket and dragged me into her house.

25

Mary Elizabeth Smith

*I*WAS FLOATING THROUGH A WARM, GRAY CLOUD when I heard a soft whisper of a song. I opened my eyes, and sitting next to me with my head resting on her lap was the same old woman I had seen before I collapsed. Her small, knotted hands were wringing out a rag into a white enamel basin filled with brownish-red water.

"Well, now, I see ya' come back from the dead, have ya'?" she said in a soft, lilting manner.

"Ah, ya' poor thing! Ya' must have come a long way to be in such a condition. Ya' paws are worn to the bone."

She poured fresh water from a jug onto my rear paws. It stung like a thousand bee stings. I cried out and tried to pull away but she held tight. The water smelled funny and made the open sores on my paws tingle.

"Thar, thar, little lad. Oh, it breaks my heart to hear ya' cry so. Ya' sound like a little baby," she said. Even through my pain, I saw her eyes turn red and glisten with tears.

"I am almost done now. Ya' will be thankin' me for this later. The Lysol may sting a wee bit, but it will fight infection. Now, there…how am I going to protect yer feet? Ya' would be chewin' any bandage right off. Now, I wonder…"

She sat quietly thinking.

"Ah, now, I know just the thing," she said.

She slowly got up, went to her cupboard, and brought out a block-shaped package. She removed the brown paper, placed the block into a pan on the stove, and lit the fire beneath it. After awhile, she came over to me with the pan and sat down on the floor again.

"Now, this is a somethin' m' father used to treat our collie, Blackie, back on the farm. He was always gettin' cuts and bruises on his pads from wearin' the sheep over the rocks," she said.

She grasped me under the crook of her arm as she dipped a spoon into the liquid that formed at the bottom of the pan. As she poured it onto the open sores, it burned worse than anything I had ever known. Worse than sharp rocks. As it cooled, a white crust formed over the top of my pads. I wriggled and struggled with each dip of her spoon but she held on. She was strong for a woman not much bigger than I was.

"There. Let us just see ya' try to lick that paraffin off. At least it will keep the dirt out and help yer feet heal," she said. "Are ya' hungry m' little darlin'?"

I barely had the energy to respond.

She brought over a bowl filled with cooked liver. I could barely swallow a few pieces before I fell back to sleep exhausted.

All through the night, the woman stayed by my side, offering me bits of food or ladling spoonfuls of water down my throat.

When morning came around, I was still sore and tired, but I felt like I had returned to the land of the living.

As I lay bundled in the blanket by the fire, I could hear the wind rattling around the house. A cold draft floated across the floor. I shivered, not so much from the cold but from the thought of going out in the weather again.

The woman was sitting in a rocking chair by the stove, a woolen blanket across her lap. I wobbled over to her. Her eyes were closed; but when I licked her hand, she opened them in surprise.

"Well now, m' beauty, how are we feelin'? A wee better?" she said stroking my head. I climbed onto her lap. I stayed there for the longest time, enjoying her touch. It had been so long since someone had treated me so kindly. She didn't seem to mind that I was dirty or that I left stains on her apron. She held me close and rocked back and forth. Again, she sang a song of another time and place. Softly and a little sad.

In the morning, I felt stronger still and my head was clear. And was I hungry! The sweet woman offered me some more food, and this time I ate my fill.

She took my paws into her hands and looked them over.

"Now, these poor feet of yours are still a long way to healin', but I do say they look a mite better. Ya' had better rest up some more," she said looking me in the eye.

I crawled across her lap once more and gave her a few whimpers and some licks across the face. It was so tempting to stay. But now that I felt better, I was eager to be on my way. I limped to the back door and scratched to be let out.

The small, bent woman stood in the doorway as she let me out. I think she expected me to simply make my mark and come back. Then she gave me a look squarely in the eyes and read my intent.

Her small, knotted hands were wringing out a rag into a white enamel basin filled with brownish-red water.

"Ya' welcome to stay, little man, but I can see ya' want to be on ya' way," she said, letting out a long sigh.

As I made the first, painful steps down the walkway, I heard another woman on the porch next door say, "Mrs. Smith, whose dog is that?"

"I do not know," Mrs. Smith said. "But I am sure whoever he belongs to must be missin' him very much. I hope he finds his way home."

26

Last Leg

I FOUND THE WAY TO THE ROAD that followed the Willamette River on the east side of Portland. The river bustled with steamships and boats of all sizes. A great din of engines, and whistles, and the smell of fish and grain filled the air.

I left the busy streets of the city behind me. The sleet had stopped, but a heavy rain continued to fall as I walked on the uneven road past the bluffs and falls of Oregon City and onward.

I was now in the valley of my childhood. Ever lush and green, moist and misty. Even in this dreary time of year, with clouds hanging low, it was paradise to me.

How I longed for some meat and a long rest. Every muscle and fiber of my body begged for me to stop. Although I could fairly taste Silverton, the pads of my bleeding feet were worn to the bone, and I had to rest often.

I found shelter wherever I could find it: barns, outbuildings, or culverts. What normally would have taken me only days to travel, took several weeks because of the condition I was in.

I passed through the small towns of Canby, Aurora, and Woodburn. Past the familiar bare, twisted vines of grapes and orchard trees, and past the empty trellises of the hop vines.

I no longer knew what I was doing beyond putting two feet in front of the other two feet. A force beyond my own drove me.

Eventually, I came to the town of Mount Angel, and I climbed to the top of the hill that swelled out of the valley floor. The rain had stopped, and the clouds were breaking apart. Rays of rain-streaked sunlight shone down upon the bare fields below me.

I could see the road that lead to Silverton. As I stood on the hill, I heard the bells of the church. I had heard this sound many times before, floating across the valley. It meant that home was not far away.

As I lay on the hilltop beneath the trees still dripping rainwater, I gathered my strength for the last few miles to home.

When I came to the valley floor, I found the road to our farm on the Abiqua River. I hobbled along beneath a canopy of bare oak trees until I came to the circular drive in front of my family's former home.

I arrived under cover of darkness when no one was about. For a few moments, I stood at the edge of the drive, watching for any sign of life in the house. I glanced toward the front porch. I half expected to see my old friend Toodles lying there. But the porch was empty.

More than anything, I wanted to be near him. I went behind the barn and found the boards that now covered Toodles' grave. I collapsed on top of them. I was with my old friend at last.

27

The Prodigal Dog

I LINGERED AT TOODLES' GRAVE for a couple of days, oblivious to the
weather and the passing of time. I didn't stir from the spot, except
to lift my heavy head and gaze through bleary eyes at the Petersons,
who spotted me on the first morning. Other than leaving me something
to eat, they left me alone. I don't believe they recognized me as the dog
once belonging to this farm. I was too weak to care. Even after a long
rest, I was still sore and tired. My legs were swollen and my feet raw
and bleeding. Now I could think more clearly. I needed to go into town
and find my family.

I left Toodles' grave and hobbled down the road toward Silverton.
Each step was more agonizing than the one before it. I wanted to run,
but I couldn't find the strength.

When I finally made it to town, I headed toward the Reo Café on
Water Street. Nothing else mattered. Not the smell of the hot dogs and
candied apples at Cunningham's Confectionary, or the sight of Clifton
Dickerson sweeping in front of his store. I had to find my family.

Just as I reached the corner of Water and Main streets, I heard a
young girl cry out.

"Look, isn't that your old dog Bobbie?" she said to another young girl
who was walking with her. I turned at the sound of my name. I looked

at the two of them across the street from me. Then I recognized Nova. My Nova!

I ran across the road and jumped up on her. I grabbed her shoulders with my paws and licked her face, crying and moaning. Nova, my sweet Nova.

"Bobbie, Bobbie, is it really you?" she said. "How did you...? After all this time...Where have you been? Look at you. You're skin and bones."

"Look at his feet, Nova. They're bleeding," the other girl said.

Nova took my front paw and gently looked at the bleeding pads.

"Bobbie, oh, Bobbie, your feet, they're worn raw. Oh, you poor thing. You must have come a long way. But how? Where have you been all this time? I can't believe it's you. Oh, Bobbie, we've missed you," Nova said hugging me. She smelled so sweet. She smelled like home.

I moaned, cried, and barked until I was hoarse. As she knelt down, I covered her face in kisses from ear to ear.

"Bobbie, Bobbie, you're home. You've come home," she said.

Nova held her arms around me for the longest time. Still crying, she finally got up.

"Frances, we have to go and tell my family right away," she said.

She led me down the street. A block away, I smelled the wonderful odors of the Reo Café. Elizabeth's apple strudel! As I rushed through the door, all conversation stopped, and the clinking of tableware ceased. I looked around at the people at the tables and the counter. Standing next to the cash register were Elizabeth and Leona.

Before Nova could say, "Look who's here," I jumped on Elizabeth.

Her mouth fell open, and for a few moments she was speechless.

"Heavens to Betsy...,"she said. "Nova, this can't be...Bobbie. It's not possible! How could he have gotten here?" she said.

"It is Bobbie, Mother. Look at him. It's Bobbie, all right. He may be mangy and skinny, but it's our Bobbie. Our Bobbie. He's come home," Nova said.

I jumped from Elizabeth to Leona and gave her a wet greeting as well. The regulars who knew me were stunned, and there wasn't a dry eye in the place.

Everyone talked at once. "Is that Bobbie? It can't be. Wasn't he lost in Indiana? He sure looks and acts like Bobbie. Look at him. He must be Bobbie."

I ran around looking for Frank. I checked behind the counter. I searched the kitchen. Where was he?

"Who are you looking for, Bobbie? Daddy? He's upstairs sleeping," Nova said.

She opened up the door that led to the back stairs. I took two steps at a time. Nova, Leona, and Elizabeth followed behind. I scratched at the door. Let me in! Let me in! Nova opened the door for me.

"Wake up, Daddy, and see who is here," she said.

Frank was lying in bed half asleep, when he heard the sound of my name. He barely had his head off the pillow before I leapt on top of him, whining, moaning, and covering his face in kisses.

"What, what on earth…Bobbie, Bobbie, is it really you?" Frank said through bleary eyes.

"It's Bobbie, Frank. Look at the way he's behaving. Who else cries like a baby when he's excited," Elizabeth said dabbing here eyes with her apron.

Frank was still groggy and looked befuddled. He held my head between his two hands and looked straight into my eyes.

"It's Bobbie all right. A little scrawny, and as dirty as a mud puddle in January, but it's him," he said.

As I sprawled across his lap, he took my paws in his hands.

"Elizabeth, look at his feet. His nails are worn to the quick, and the pads are bleeding. Why, this one is worn to the bone. It looks as if our Bobbie has walked all the way back from Indiana."

"Oh, Frank, he couldn't have. How on earth…?" she said.

"How else did he make it home? He must have walked. But how did he find his way? Bobbie, where have you been? We thought we would never see you again. You are either the cleverest dog in the world or the luckiest," he said.

I whined as I leaned into him. We stayed close for a long time. I never wanted to move. Everyone gathered around the bed and gave me a full dose of affection. They offered me water and food, but fatigue overtook me and I collapsed into a deep sleep next to Frank.

I didn't dream of the farm on the Abiqua, or of the delicious smells of the Reo, or of a long road leading to forever. I didn't dream at all. I had come home at last.

28

Not So Quiet on the Western Front

WHEN I AWOKE, FRANK HAD DOZED OFF by my side. I woke him up with some licks on his feet that were sticking out from underneath the covers. He slowly opened his eyes and spotted me on the edge of the bed staring at him.

"I still can't believe it's really you, Bobbie. I thought I might have dreamed this whole thing. I would never, never have thought it possible if you weren't right here before my eyes," he said stroking my head.

He then led me downstairs to the Reo's kitchen. With a whistle and a smile, he rewarded me with a pint of fresh cream, and the best sirloin steak in the house. But I was too tired to eat it all.

"What's the matter, Bobbie? Steak not good enough for you?" Frank asked.

I rolled over on my back and held my paws in the air. I saw Frank's eyes glisten with tears.

"The best thing for you is a long rest and some nursing," he said.

He led me down to my old place in the basement and made a bed for me. I collapsed on my wonderful, familiar-smelling blankets. I didn't move for three days and three nights. Whenever anyone tried to rouse me, I just rolled over on my back and showed my torn paws, and I was left alone.

Nova sat by my side and offered me food. But I only ate small amounts. I had gotten used to eating raw food, so it took me awhile to get used to cooked food again.

While I lay in my bed, shut off from the world, the news of my return spread like a grass fire through the valley.

One day Frank came into the Reo Café with a copy of the Silverton newspaper.

"Listen up everybody, there's a column about Bobbie in the *Appeal*.

'Dog Returns After Long Trip. "Bob" the big Scotch collie—belonging to Mr. and Mrs. G.F. Brazier proprietors of the Reo Lunch Restaurant in this city—surprised his owners one day this week when he showed up at their place of business after an absence of about six months…' It goes on to say how he was lost in Indiana last summer. Gosh, I knew this was news, but I didn't think we would have made the front page. That's one for the scrapbook, isn't it, Elizabeth?" he said.

The next thing we knew, people came from all over the county to eat at the restaurant and to catch a glimpse of the famous "Bobbie, the Wonder Dog."

Like pilgrims to a shrine, the locals came to gawk at me and boast that they knew me when. Soon it was standing room only. People stood in line and pressed their faces to the window to peer inside.

"Can you see the dog? Where's Bobbie? Is he here yet?" they would all say.

Reporters, with pad and pencil, interviewed Frank, and soon hundreds of newspapers and magazines across the country printed an account of my story. People read about me in the *Christian Science Monitor*, the *New York Herald*, the *Chicago Tribune* and many others. The *Oregonian* proposed I be crowned King of the Hobos.

The demand for my picture became so great that when I recuperated, Frank took me to the Drake Brothers photography studio in town. I posed for a number of photographs on top of a piano bench and in front of a backdrop of painted trees. I posed across Frank's lap as well as with Elizabeth and Nova. They produced these in quantity, so that all the people who requested them could have a copy.

Soon thereafter, Frank and Elizabeth received letters from doglovers all over the country and beyond, asking for details or requesting a photo. I received letters from businessmen, housewives, military men, and, of course, children. Many wrote to express their admiration or to compare me to their own "Wonder Dog." Others wrote poetic tributes or short stories. Some were addressed simply: "Bobbie, the Wonder Dog, Silverton, Oregon," or "Silverton Bobbie," or "Bobbie, the dog that walked across the Country," or even "Bobbie Brazier, the collie dog who crossed seven states alone to get home, Silverton, Oregon." The post office never failed to deliver any mail that had any variation of my name on it. Frank and Elizabeth felt compelled to answer them all. They had to retell my story so many times, Frank finally typed it out and had it printed in quantity, so that it could be sent out to all the interested people.

Every day, Nova greeted the mailman at the door of the Reo.

"Look here, everybody! More Bobbie mail! Why, there are letters from New York, Pennsylvania, Indiana...all over the country. How on earth could people know about Bobbie?" she said.

"The wire services must be picking up on the story. Who would have ever thought it would get this big?" Elizabeth said shuffling through the stack of letters.

Nova opened one of the letters and read it aloud.

"Dear Bobbie, I suppose you will be surprised to get a letter. I am going to tell you why I am writing to you, but first I'd better tell you who I am. I am sure you are anxious to know.

"I am a boy twelve years old and I live in Bloomington, and I go to school here too. I am in the sixth grade.

"I love dogs more than anything else in the world. I have a little dog whose name is 'Queen.' She is a fox terrier. She is an awfully smart little dog.

"I got a little bull dog for Christmas but she died about a month after I got her. I called her 'Bubbles.' I sure did cry too even if I am a boy.

"But Bobbie I want to tell you what a smart doggie I think you are. I read the piece in the paper about you getting lost in Iowa and walking to Indiana then clear back to Oregon. Bobbie I just wish I could give you a great big hug. I think you are the most wonderfulst dog I ever heard to tell of to be so smart as to go all that way home alone. I bet you have a good home Bobbie or you'd never would have tried to walk all the way back and I bet the people who own you love you more than ever. I've never even seen you and I am sure I love you and I wish you were my dog. I'd be so good to you and I'd give you lots to eat and you could sleep in the house. But I'm sure Mr. and Mrs. Brazier love you too much to ever sell you to anybody for I know if you were my doggie I'd not sell you for all the money there was for I'd love you so much. We'd be great pals for I believe you would like me too. Do you think you would?

"Bobbie I wonder if Mrs. Brazier would send me a picture of you. It

127

would make me so happy and you know I would keep it forever if they will. I'll send you a picture of my doggie and by return mail and you can look at it and say that little boy wrote me a letter and he thinks I'm the nicest and smartest dog he every heard of. Well, I hope your master will be so kind as to read this letter to you. If he will I just know you will understand it and Bobbie, please, won't you have them send me your picture and I will send you mine right away. Goodbye Bobbie, I wish I knew you. Sincerely, Howard Everingham, Bloomington, Illinois."

"Oh, isn't that just the sweetest thing? Why, Bobbie, you're famous! They'll be no living with you now!" Nova said.

So much happened within those first few days and weeks of my return. One day, Frank received a letter from Colonel Hofer, the president of the Oregon Humane Society in Portland. He wrote that he was interested in my story and wanted to conduct an investigation. He came down to Silverton to meet with Frank at the Reo Café.

"Mr. Brazier, first of all, I am curious about the day Bobbie got lost. Exactly what happened? What did you do?" Colonel Hofer said.

"Well, when we first got to Wolcott, I dropped Mrs. Brazier off at our friend's house, and then I drove with Bobbie to a service station to have the Overland's carburetor adjusted. Bobbie jumped off and started to nose around as he usually does, when a bulldog took off after him. Bobbie disappeared from sight, but I didn't think much of it. He has always been able to take care of himself, and I figured he would show up eventually. Well, when I got ready to leave there was no sight of him. I honked the horn, as that usually got him running. Then, I drove around town until midnight looking for him, but still no Bobbie. The first thing I did the next morning was to call all around town to see if anyone had spotted him. I even called the local newspaper, and luckily the editor was able to post an ad in the current issue. We stayed around an extra couple of days in hopes we would hear something. Then we had to continue on our way to Bluffton, Indiana, and Ohio. We left word with our friends in Wolcott to notify us if Bobbie should turn up. For three weeks, we visited family in the Midwest and then returned to Wolcott on the way back. But still no word of Bobbie.

"When we returned to Silverton and didn't hear anything, we figured Bobbie was gone for good. We were broken-hearted. Nova especially was torn apart. They were best pals. So, as you can see, we were just as surprised as everyone to see Bobbie show up at our doorstep six months later. Since I talked with you last, we have gotten quite a few more letters about Bobbie. The ones in this pile are from people who claim that they sheltered a dog that looked very much like him. I've reviewed them, and I think there is a definite possibility that the dog they talk about is Bobbie. Tell me what you think," Frank said handing them to Colonel Hofer.

Colonel Hofer looked over the letters and read portions of them aloud.

"'Dear Sir: The enclosed picture appeared in an Indianapolis paper recently and I am wondering if I did not make the acquaintance of Bobbie last summer at my shack on the Tippecanoe River.

"I was sitting under a tree one summer day, when I heard a splashing in the river and running up the hill came a collie dog which I knew at once was seeking his master. He ran rapidly up the path past my cottage and out into the road, which is a sort of private lane leading to but two places...

"Much to our surprise, the dog came back several days later, very tired. We petted and fed him. We took care of him and wanted very much to keep him, but we found him gone in the morning.

"It was easy to see that he was distressed and in search of someone.

"Whether it was your Bobbie or not, I am well pleased that you got your dog back. Nothing is more sorrowful than a dog longing for his master. I hope his toenails are growing again. Very truly yours, Sarah S. Pratt.'"

"Now, Mrs. Pratt was at a summer camp on the Tippecanoe River and that is not very far from Wolcott, where we first lost Bobbie. But there are other letters from people in different parts of the country," Frank said.

"Here's one from a Mrs. Plumb in Des Moines," Colonel Hofer said.

"'My dear Mrs. Brazier, I was greatly interested in an article appearing in the April number of *Moral Welfare* concerning the exploits of a collie 'Bob' which you own. The picture so closely resembles a collie which we had the pleasure of entertaining for a few months during the summer and fall of *1923*, that I am prompted to write you in the hope of establishing his identity.

"He made his appearance during the night and, finding my nephew sleeping on the porch, offered his paw to shake hands, after which he quietly went to sleep. In the morning—after shaking hands with the family and receiving his breakfast—he departed in the direction of the tourist camp (which is only a few blocks from our house) but in an hour or so came back to us and took up his abode. Although we were very fond of him, no effort was made to keep him.

"Almost every day he made the trip in the direction of the tourist camp, which led us to believe he had been lost from there. We tried out different names, and found the name Bob seemed to suit him best.

"While with us, he disappeared for several days at one time, and upon his return we found the heavy strap collar had been removed, and a much lighter one substituted to which a fragment of rope was attached, showing plainly that someone had tried to keep him.

"The latter part of November, 1923 (the day after Thanksgiving to be exact) he again disappeared and has never returned to us.

"It is unnecessary to say that we deeply regretted losing him, but have always hoped he found his way back to his own people.

"Am enclosing a couple of Kodaks showing the markings of the face but am sorry they do not show the entire body.

"If the above data corresponds with what you already know of the dog's trip—and you must have reason to believe that the two Bobs are one and the same collie—I would be glad to hear from you. Ida Plumb.'"

"Here's a letter from a Carrie Abbee in Denver who claims seeing him in December. Listen to this," he said.

" '…He was a very nice behaved dog and seemed very tired, in fact exhausted, was dusty and had burrs in his hair. We spoke of his being so tired, and that he looked as though he had a long hike, although he was in good condition. We hoped he would stay with us, but in the morning he did not even wait for his breakfast.'"

"Well, Mr. Brazier. This is impressive. What I'll do is take these letters and do some investigating. It certainly looks like all of these people believe that the dog they encountered was Bobbie," Colonel Hofer said.

About a week later, Colonel Hofer reported to Frank.

"Mr. Brazier, I have contacted these people and they were able to verify that they had seen a dog very much like Bobbie. By their description of his behavior, the scar above his eye, his slight limp from being run over by that tractor, and his missing teeth, I am convinced that he is the same dog in question. In addition, we have also heard from several garage owners in various states that recalled seeing Bobbie and offering him a meal. It appears that your Bobbie did indeed find his way home by himself. It's the most remarkable thing I have ever heard of," he said.

Soon thereafter, the Oregon Humane Society presented an engraved silver medal to me in a ceremony in front of the grade school in Silverton. I posed with Frank, Elizabeth, the mayor, Colonel Hofer, and a large group of students while a photographer took our picture. The engraving on the medal stated that I was lost in Iowa, not Indiana. But I guess it's the thought that counts. In addition, the schoolchildren submitted a petition to the mayor to grant me free reign of the city, which I pretty much had anyway.

This was only the beginning of a number of personal appearances I was to make that spring and summer. Early on, people came out of the woodwork to take advantage of Frank and Elizabeth and to line their own pockets.

Two Portland businessmen named Crossley and McFadden came to Silverton and approached Frank about having me appear at the annual Portland Home Show. They were the promoters of the show and they wanted Frank and me for a weeks' worth of appearances at the auditorium.

"Bobbie will be the star attraction. The theme of this year's show is 'Love of Home,' and who but Bobbie symbolizes those sentiments so perfectly? Thousands of people will see him. And this is only the beginning. I guarantee it. I see big things in Bobbie's future and yours, Mr. Brazier," Mr. Crossley said shaking Frank's hand.

At the opening ceremonies of the Home Beautiful Show, Frank and I stood before a large crowd of people, while Mr. Crossley made a long-winded speech about loyalty, faithfulness, and the importance of home, and then presented me with a custom-made leather harness with an engraved silver plate made by the Jaeger Brothers of Portland. The icing on the cake was when he unveiled a red-and-yellow dog-sized bungalow house, complete with windows, silk curtains, and a solid oak door with a glass doorknob.

"Mr. Brazier, on behalf of the Portland Realty Board, it is my honor to present you with the deed to Bobbie's castle," he said.

There was a thunderous round of applause, while I acted suitably enthusiastic. I made a show of pushing the door open and walking around inside and sticking my head out the windows, while photographers snapped pictures.

People flocked to the home show like ducks to a pond. On the first day of the show, about fifty thousand people came by to see my "castle" and me. I was amazed as to the number of people that could fit under one roof. There were long aisles of booths, and tables with displays of the newest electric toasters, vacuum cleaners, and ironing machines that promised to relieve the housewife of her life of drudgery.

It was an exhausting day. My eyes became blurry from all the camera flashbulbs shooting off in my face. I became so sore from all the people clamoring to pet me that, by the second day, they had to erect a fence to keep the people at a distance.

By the last day of the show, I'd had my fill. I just wanted to go back to Silverton where I could nap in peace. Near the end of the day, there was still a large crowd waiting in line to see me. I was counting the minutes until it was over, when suddenly there was a commotion at the back of the line.

Against the protest of a number of tired-looking parents, Mr. Crossley was escorting someone to the front of the line. As they shuffled closer through the crowd, I recognized the woman on his arm as the same white-haired woman who had nursed me in Portland just a couple of months before.

By the astonished look on her face, I knew she recognized me as well. As she came through the fencing, I moaned and whined. When she got near, I put my paws on her frail shoulders and licked the tears from her crinkled cheeks. Everyone was wondering what all the fuss was about.

"Yes, yes, this is the same dog that came to m' back door last January. I will swear on m' rosary. Only then, he was a pitiful sight. So skinny and weak, and his poor paws were all bloody. Now, I tell ya', it just broke m' heart. He stayed with me for a couple of nights, but then he was on his way. I have been thinking about him ever since. I even said a prayer to Saint Francis and Saint Christopher that he would be safe with his family. I will be guessing m' prayers were answered," she said.

It was Mrs. Smith's testimony that impressed so many people at the home show as well as those who read about it in the paper later. In the eyes of Frank, Colonel Hofer, and Mr. Crossley, this further proved that I did make my way home from Indiana on my own. I guess my word was simply not good enough for them. But then, they never listened to me anyway.

The next major event after the home show was transporting my castle and me down to Silverton. Mr. Crossley and Mr. McFadden saw to it that this was also a newsworthy event. Reporters and photographers from the *Oregonian* and the *Oregon Journal* followed along to cover the story. I rode with my house on the back of a large flatbed truck that was decorated with red, white, and blue bunting and flags. People lined the streets of all the towns from Portland to Silverton.

As much as I enjoyed being the center of attention, I was still tired from my long trip and from all the people who petted me at the home show. I just wanted things to get back to normal, back to several naps a day. However, Frank was so proud of me and he loved to entertain the crowds. I tried not to let on that I just wanted to go home.

Eventually, they placed my castle in front of the Reo Café where it became a regular fixture. The children of Silverton would come by on their way home from school just to pet me. They considered me as much their dog as my family did.

29

The Price of Fame

THE WEEKS AND MONTHS OF THAT SUMMER are a blur to me. Frank and I made so many personal appearances I lost track. We appeared at county and state fairs, theaters, and auditoriums. I received flowers in glass cases from Australia, gifts too numerous to mention. They adorned me with medals and presented me with keys to cities. There were long, tiresome ceremonies and speeches by people who pretended they knew me when.

Soon, articles appeared in major magazines such as *Forest and Stream*, *National Geographic*, and *Popular Mechanics*. The famous dog-writer Albert Payson Terhune wrote about me in a collection of true-dog stories.

One of the other major features that came out with my story was in the column "Ripley's Believe It or Not." At the time, Mr. Ripley offered a ten thousand dollar reward to anyone who could disprove one of his stories. Since no one came forward to do so, people believed my story.

There was so much interest from the public regarding my story, it seemed a day didn't go by where Frank and I weren't appearing somewhere or having another writer, reporter, or curiosity-seeker drop by.

Out of the throng of human characters that frequented our doorstep, Dr. Rhinehouse of the Department of Parapsychology at Duke University was the only one who attempted to interview me directly. He contacted Frank and made a special trip to Silverton just to meet me.

Dr. Rhinehouse conducted a number of what he called "experiments" with me in the parlor of the apartment above the Reo. One of the experiments involved two sets of large cards with pictures printed on them. He laid one set out on a low table in front of me, and the other he held in his hand. He picked one card up, stared at it intently, and then waited for me to do something. It took me awhile to understand that he wanted me to point to one of the cards on the table. Therefore, after a few trials and errors, I lifted my paw and randomly patted one of the cards. He would get very excited like a child. His eyes widened and he squirmed in his seat uttering, "Yes, yes, very good, Bobbie, very good." This went on for about half an hour.

We played several other games with a varying degree of success. I really didn't understand the purpose of it all. But then again, people have an odd sense of fun.

When Dr. Rhinehouse had finished with his games, he had a long talk with Frank and Elizabeth about something he called "extra sensory perception" or "the sixth sense."

Despite a sincere effort on my behalf, I am afraid I was a disappointment to Dr. Rhinehouse. Even though I learned to point to cards with pictures on them, I didn't point to the right ones at the right time. If he'd only told me what he needed. I'm not a mind-reader.

However, interest in my story didn't end with Dr. Rhinehouse. Later that spring, Mr. Crossley suggested that someone should write a book about me.

He didn't waste any time in contacting a well known author of animal stories, Charles Alexander of Albany, Oregon.

Mr. Alexander came to our house a number of times and interviewed Frank and Elizabeth and visited with me. Eventually, he wrote *Bobbie, a Great Collie*. It had reasonable success at first, but then interest waned as quickly as the publicity about me did. It was a good book— as books by people go. But it didn't tell the whole story as I would have liked.

About the same time that Mr. Alexander was researching the book, an unusual coincidence occurred. I was walking with Frank in a field not far from our home, when I spotted a hobo camp near some railroad tracks. Two men were sitting by the campsite. At first, I didn't think anything of them; but then, upon closer view, I noticed that one of the men looked familiar to me. It took me a few moments to realize where

I had seen him. He was the same Tom that fed me and shared his campfire back in Indianapolis.

I greeted him with a bounding leap, a great many licks, and cries of joy. At first he looked confused, but then stunned after he realized who I was.

After a thorough wet greeting, Tom and Frank introduced themselves.

"Do you know my dog? It seems he knows you. Have you two met before?" Frank said.

"Why, I wouldn't believe it if I wasn't seeing it for myself," Tom said. "I saw this same dog in a campsite in Indianapolis. He showed up one night after swimming the White River. He just walked up to the campfire and made himself at home. A friendly fellow. Had real good manners. Better than my own, ha. I always wondered what happened to him. One day, he just disappeared. Don't mind saying, I got a bit attached to him," Tom said.

"You mean to tell me you saw him in Indianapolis? I can't believe it. He disappeared on us, while my wife and I were visiting friends in Wolcott. That's in northern Indiana. I wonder why he wandered that far south. You're sure this is the same dog?" Frank said.

"Yep, my memory isn't as good as it used to be, but I'd never forget that face," Tom said. "How did you ever find him?"

"We didn't find him, he found us. He showed up at the door of our business here in Oregon just last February. He was missing for six months. It was something of a miracle. Somewhat like now. What are the odds that the two of you would see each other again in another part of the country?" Frank said.

"Well, I've seen some strange things in my life. But nothing like this. He must be pretty smart to find his way back home. Hey fella, glad to know you made it home," Tom said. "You can be sure I won't forget you."

Frank said goodbye to Tom, who looked rather sad, as if he had found a friend, just to lose him again.

30
The Call of the West

I N THE SUMMER OF 1924, about the same time Mr. Alexander was writing the book, Mr. Crossley contacted Frank and proposed making a film based on my cross-country trip. Crossley and his partners formed a company called the Columbia Theatre Syndicate, and they wanted their first venture to be a film about me.

"I believe Bobbie could be as big a star as Strongheart or Rin Tin Tin. Just you wait and see, Mr. Brazier. He has what it takes. We have the whole story planned out. The working title is *Bobbie, the Wonder Dog*. That'll catch their interest. There isn't a dog-lover out there who wouldn't want to see this film," Mr. Crossley said.

In order to devote more time to the making of the movie, Frank sold the Reo Café and moved the family to Salem. To me, this was a great disappointment, as I could no longer wander about town at will, and I missed the familiar haunts of Silverton.

I'm afraid Frank got caught up in all the excitement and thought there might be a way to make money out of the movie deal. He trusted Mr. Crossley and the others of the Columbia Picture Syndicate and thought they were headed for the big time.

However, I learned you can't always trust artistic types. They seem to have a rather high opinion of their ideas no matter where they might have gotten them. When you get a bunch of people together, they refuse to act as a pack. They all want to do things their way and end up working against each other.

At the production meeting for the movie, I never saw so much squabbling in all my life. You would have thought someone had thrown a big, juicy bone into the middle of them, and they all went after it at the same time. Eventually, they came up with a rough storyline, nothing of which was based on reality.

A small crew of local actors played multiple characters in the movie. By utilizing various changes of costume, hairpieces, false mustaches, and beards, for example, the man who played the policeman also played the dog catcher and the itinerant peddler. This helped the production company because then not so many actors had to be hired for the film. Anyone else who wanted to be in the movie just had to show up, and the director put them to use playing background people.

There was also a part in the film for a little boy to play my master and best friend. Since this was such a central character, the director held auditions to find just the "right" little boy.

The director made his decision based on how well the boys took direction and how they conveyed emotion. I can't even tell you how many times they had me run a scene with another contender. Each boy was asked to pretend that he'd seen me for the first time after my return to Silverton. He was to be on the street corner joking with friends. I would come down the street bedraggled, exhausted, and on my last legs. One of the boys would see me and recognize me. "Isn't that your dog, Bobbie?" he was supposed to say. When I'd hear the word "Bobbie" I would recognize my young master, run to him, and have a tearful reunion. Should have been simple enough, you'd think. However, I had to play this same scene over and over for dozens of young boys large and small, slow and quick. I personally never gave less than one hundred percent. But honestly, playing against some of these young boys was like chewing on chalk. Lifeless and tasteless.

If trying to turn these ragamuffins into thespians wasn't hard enough, there were the minions of parents who accompanied the auditioners. They stood on the sidelines, often coaching their offspring in the middle of the audition and generally making a nuisance of themselves. If there is anything worse than a theater brat it is his mother. They picked at their children like mother birds grooming the ruffled feathers of a fledgling, adjusting lapels, knickers, and socks. Applying spit to cowlicks. Producing all sorts of grooming implements, lotions, brushes, and pomades. These preparations often took longer than the audition.

After a day and a half of agonizing tryouts and dozens of aspirants, the director finally hired a dark-haired, freckle-faced boy named Martin Marks.

He wasn't all starry-eyed about fame like the others, so we got along. He also knew how to take direction and follow my lead.

Frank and Elizabeth played themselves in the movie but really were only in one scene at the opening. Leona and Nova appeared only as extras. Nova was especially miffed at being relegated to a minor role, and that the main character was a boy. The director said that the public would respond to the story of a boy and his dog better than a girl and her dog. "There's a burnt out light bulb for every broken heart on Broadway," he said. That's just the way things were done in the movie world.

None of us had ever been involved in making a movie before. Even the director didn't really know what he was doing. The only ones with any real experience were the scriptwriter, Mr. Chambers, and the cameraman, Mr. Heaton. Both of them had some previous work in films, mostly newsreels and documentaries. But neither of them had worked on a dramatic production before.

The script—if you could call it that—had almost no basis in reality. The actors hammed it up to the point of distraction, but I still stole most of the scenes without as much as a flick of my tail. Thankfully, the little boy, Martin, was able to put in a fine, natural performance.

One of the more tedious pieces of business involved a scene between the itinerant peddler and me. In the scene, the peddler persuades the little boy (Martin) to sell his dog (me). The peddler then puts a piece of rope around my neck, ties me to his wagon, and leaves me there alone.

The idea was that I was supposed to bark furiously and chew through the rope to set myself free.

Frank suggested that he play the harmonica to provoke me to bark, as it always worked in the past.

Well, I barked on cue, but chewing through the rope did not go according to plan. We had to re-shoot the scene a number of times and, after about the third or fourth take, I had just had my fill of it and wanted to bite someone.

Then, one of the crew got the bright idea to tie the end of the rope to a wiener, which was then tied to another piece of string attached to the wagon. They figured I would eat the wiener and set myself free.

Well, this did not go according to plan either. It was obvious I was eating a wiener and not chewing through the rope. Therefore, we had to film the scene a few more times at different angles so it was not so obvious.

Between the man playing the harmonica, the director, and Frank shouting "Get the wiener, Bobbie, get the wiener," I became very frustrated and had my first and last tantrum. Not only did I get the wiener, but I grabbed the entire string of wiener links. The peddler took hold of the other end and, for a few minutes, we ended up in a wiener tug of war. But I proved too strong for him, and he lost his grip.

Frank, the director, the cameraman, and several extras chased me down the street trying to get a hold of me, but I was too fast for them. Needless to say, we ran out of time and out of wieners that day.

Despite the setbacks and lack of experience on everyone's behalf, it took less than six weeks to make the movie, and we ended up with two reels of film.

That summer the movie was released under the final title *The Call of the West*. It premiered at the Columbia Theater in Portland and then toured to smaller towns as well.

The movie played for three days at the Bligh Theatre in Salem. Frank and I arrived and stood outside the entrance. Frank was reading a poster pasted to a billboard out front. "Bobbie, the Wonder Dog from Silverton in the motion picture *The Call of the West*. Oh, yes! The dog will be here himself with his master, too."

"See that, Bobbie, you are a big draw now," he said.

When we entered the theater and came on stage, the children in the audience went crazy, jumping up and down in their seats, squealing and clapping. We were introduced by another man on stage, and then Frank told a brief version of my adventure and answered questions from the audience. Toward the end of the presentation, he brought out his harmonica, and played it for the children. This was not so much because he could play the harmonica but to get me to sing. To my frustration, the children loved it and asked for an encore. My impatience was clear, as my nails clicked and tapped on the wooden floor of the stage.

"You see boys and girls, not only does Bobbie sing, but he tap-dances too!" Frank announced. This only made them laugh even louder. I thought it would never end.

The film was not promoted as well as Frank would have liked. I think he was disappointed, because he ended up losing money.

Other movie companies approached Frank about doing another film with a wider distribution, but nothing really came of it. I think he became a little disillusioned with "artistic" types. They were good at talking up a project, but most of it was just smoke and mirrors. I think with a better writer, director, and producer the film could have had a better following. I also think that a better job of promoting the film could have been done. But then, that is only one dog's opinion. Both Frank and I had a taste of show business, and had our fill of it.

I was looking forward to our lives getting back to normal.

31

All Bobbies

WELL, THINGS DID NOT QUIET DOWN as I would have hoped. We all settled into a large home on Commercial Street in Salem. Frank got involved in a small mercantile business in town but still made time for special appearances with me. However, once the movie and the book were released, and the initial enthusiasm died down, there was less demand for such appearances.

There were still many requests by mail for photographs or for my paw print, and for more information on my exploits. Frank and Elizabeth found time to answer them all.

There was an offer from a man to breed me with their female dog.

"I have never used a stud dog that was not registered. In this case, I would gladly break the rule and breed my lady to Bobbie. My objective in using Bobbie would be to improve the long distance field quality of my dogs. Mr. J. C. Fairchild, Redlands, California."

Of course, I had no say in the matter.

There were many requests by people from all over the country wanting to purchase a puppy by the famous "Wonder Dog of Silverton." Because of this, Frank and Elizabeth found a mate for me locally.

Her name was Tippy. She was a Scotch collie from Salem. Her coloring and form were very similar to my own mother, Lady. Since she was a pure-bred from a strong lineage, they felt that she would be a

All Bobbies

suitable mother to bear such famous offspring. However, I am not sure she knew what she was getting into.

Once the news hit the papers that I was a father, Frank was flooded with requests from people who were willing to pay top money for one of the pups.

Frank had to be very discriminating with regard to who would be eligible. For the first six weeks or so Tippy, the puppies, and I were prominently displayed on the front lawn of our home in Salem along with our castle. A fence was erected around the house, so that the pups could have plenty of playing room, and that we could be easily viewed by the public. Our photographs appeared in all the local papers and beyond.

Tippy gave birth to sixteen puppies—all boys—but five of them died shortly after their birth. This, of course, was very sad for all of us, including the many people who longed for one of the pups. They were a fine-looking group of boys if I do say so myself. Full of life as all pups are. They took to the spotlight like flies to flypaper.

Once they were of age, one by one, Frank found homes for them. I do not know all of the people who eventually adopted them. Frank offered them to a number of people, some who were from this story. The Plumb family in Iowa was offered one of my boys because of all

the care they had given me during my stay in Des Moines. I also know they offered a puppy to the folks in The Dalles, Oregon, who took me in, and to the writer, Mr. Alexander. One of the pups was given to Mrs. Smith, the lady from Portland who nursed me. She named it "Pippy." Shortly after, she wrote to us.

"I write to tell you that Pippy, our little dog, is no more. He ran out in the street and got run over and killed. I am so sorry. I do not want any more little pets. My little dog is gone."

Some of the other pups did not survive for long, as they came down with distemper.

We lost track of our other puppies after they were adopted and never learned their fate. This is how it is with dogs.

However, Frank and Elizabeth kept one of the pups as their own. They named him "Pal." He is the largest of the boys and resembles me the most in coloring and personality. Tippy and I are very proud of him. He is good company for me now that all the other boys are gone, and Tippy has returned to live with her family.

Everything quieted down after the pups were born and adopted. Leona married Clifton Dickerson of Dickerson's store within a year of my return. They moved back to Silverton to live.

So now, it is just Frank and Elizabeth, Nova, Pal, and I living in our big house in Salem.

I don't miss all the activity and excitement. I found it all rather tiring. Now, all I want to do is lie out on the front porch and take walks with Frank and Pal. We go to the country twice a day for a run. Pal and I have a great time chasing rabbits and gophers. I am not as fast I used to be. My old tractor injury slows me down. (That was the only time I ever got hurt taking a nap.) Cold, icy weather makes my feet throb. And every now and then my stomach gets queasy. I haven't quite gotten used to eating cooked food again. But I'm not complaining. My other senses are intact. I can still smell a gopher from a mile away and hear it sneeze.

I look back on my life, and I figure I could have done without all the excitement. I was happy with the way things were and couldn't have asked for a better place to grow up than Silverton. Of all the places I traveled, from desert to plain, valley to mountain, I liked Silverton best.

So now, I am content to stay put. I sniff things. I take time to mark the roses. I no longer wander much farther than the road at the end of the path. Life is deliciously boring, which suits me just fine.

Epilogue
As Told by Pal

I'M NOT THE STORYTELLER DAD WAS. However, since he is no longer with us, I feel it is important that everyone know of his final days. It is true that Dad was not the same dog after he returned from his cross-country trip. Of course, I didn't know him before his trip to make a comparison. I only know what other people said about him. While he would always romp and play with me and my brothers, he tired easily. Still, he was a good dad and we never lacked for attention.

Dad lived for two years after I was born. I am grateful we had that long together. Not many dogs get to stay with their parents after they are born. I don't remember too much about the excitement our birth caused, except for the times when the photographers came around and flashed flashbulbs in our faces. This was, of course, after our eyes were opened. Elizabeth and my mother, Tippy, wouldn't have allowed such an intrusion on newly-born pups.

I remember people coming by and visiting us out in front of the house on Commercial Street in Salem. Dad was very protective of us yet friendly to all who came by, especially the children. He handled the crowds like a professional.

It wasn't until later that I understood what all the excitement was about and why Dad was famous. I also became aware of the heavy responsibility of being his son. I became the focus of attention for a long time after. Since I was the only one of my brothers that was kept with the family, I was called upon to pose for pictures with Dad and to make personal appearances. At first, I found all the attention exciting. But I could see that Dad enjoyed it less and less. He preferred to stay close to home. His only real enjoyment was going for walks with Frank and me.

Dad became ill in the spring of 1927, and Frank took him to the Rose City Veterinary Hospital in Portland, where he stayed for three weeks. Dad had lost his appetite. Dr. Huthman tempted him with malted milk to which he became partial, but then he lost interest. Sometimes he would try a little raw meat, as that was what he had gotten used to eating.

Even in his illness, he was a celebrity, and his hospital stay made the papers. He made a brave effort to appear jovial as he posed for photographs from the kennel in the hospital.

Various friends visited him while he was there including Winifred Pickering, the lady who wrote the article about him in *Everybody's Magazine*.

Soon after, our family received letters from people all over urging Frank to take my father home and not keep him at the veterinary hospital.

"Let his eyes rest on his master as they close in death," said one writer.

Other letters poured in with advice on various treatments and remedies. One writer recommended flaxseed tea and peppermint.

"It heals the stomach and keeps the bowels open," the letter said.

Another suggested Christian Science as a way to cure his illness.

He slowly got worse, even though he was taken out each day and tried to play with the other dogs. The doctor said he was "game to the end."

However, after several trips back and forth, and despite constant care in the hospital, Dad died. In the quiet hours of the early morning of April 4, 1927, he went to sleep on the hay inside his wooden kennel and never woke up. Dr. Huthman wired Frank a telegram to let him know.

What actually caused Dad's death is not clear. The doctor thought it was a combination of things. He determined that Dad had aged ten years due to the hardships of his travels, and that the pneumonia he contracted in Iowa weakened him further. The doctor also felt that his diet, which was heavy on raw meat and bones, had caused ulcers in his stomach. He suspected that Dad had gotten ptomaine poisoning from a bad bone, and that hemorrhaging ulcers were what ultimately killed him. Therefore, in many ways, it was a bone that did him in.

The newspapers carried the news of his death and condolences, flowers, and gifts started to flood in. The Humane Society sent a sympathetic telegram by carrier pigeon.

Dad's funeral was held on the grounds of the Oregon Humane Society in Portland. The weather remained unpredictable. It rained cats and dogs and then Great Danes, as Dad used to say. Everyone huddled at the entrance beneath a sea of black umbrellas. Soon, a long, black automobile pulled into the curved driveway in front of the building. Several somber-looking men in dark overcoats and pork-pie hats gathered by the back of the auto and opened up the back doors. Inside was a small, wooden casket with plain, brass handles. I knew without anyone telling me that Dad was inside. How small the casket was. Somehow, Dad always seemed larger than life to me.

The four men carried the casket underneath a metal archway to the animal cemetery, and to a spot near some large cedar trees. Here, they lowered the casket into a hole that had been dug earlier. The people decorated the casket with flowers and fern fronds.

Nova's face was pinched and red from crying as she laid a bouquet of carnations on the grave.

"These are from Pal, Bobbie," she said.

Frank stood by quietly with his hat in his hands and looked as if he was trying hard not to cry. Everyone gathered around and listened solemnly to Mr. Crossley and others give their long-winded speeches. I didn't stick around.

Instead, I wandered among a sea of knees. I recognized Mr. Alexander who wrote the book about Dad. He looked tired and a bit haggard. I overheard him say to Frank that he hoped that the sales of the books might pick up now that Bobbie had passed on. I thought that was not in very good taste, but then he was only human.

Mayor Baker and Colonel Hofer, Mrs. Swanton and Frances Blakely of the Humane Society, as well as members of the press all attended. Leona was there with her husband, Clifton Dickerson, and their little girl, Vades. In total, there were two hundred people and me at the funeral.

Standing apart from the rest was a group of people whispering among themselves. One lady wore a big, black hat with the two wings of a black bird pinned on top. Why anyone would want to wear a dead bird on their head, I don't know. I never killed a bird myself. Although my father said he killed a number of birds on his trek; he told me the wings were the least-tasty part. Certainly not worth wearing around on one's head.

This woman was whispering into another woman's ear.

"Of course, there are those who claimed it was all a big hoax. I heard that Frank Brazier staged the whole thing as a publicity stunt for their restaurant. Some say that Bobbie was on the farm where they used to live the whole time. I've even heard Mr. Dickerson, the Brazier's son-in-law, claim that Bobbie was so dumb he couldn't have found his tail if he were downwind of it," she whispered.

"But what about all the letters from the people who saw him? What about him showing up at the restaurant all dirty and matted with his feet worn raw?" the other woman said.

The bird lady said, "The letters probably were sent by friends of the Braziers. It's easy enough to make a dog look like it's been on the road. Come on now, could a dog, any dog, possibly travel all by himself over two thousand miles across the country? Over the mountains in the middle of winter? Either he had a lot of help, or it was all a big story made up by some very imaginative minds. I just don't believe it. I think some people were looking for a way to strike it rich."

"But what about Colonel Hofer and Mr. Crossley of the Humane Society, or Mr. Alexander? They also looked into it and verified everything," the other woman said.

The bird lady pursed her lips and rolled her eyes.

"Oh, they all had something to gain by maintaining it was true. Lots of free publicity for the Humane Society. Crossley got thousands of people to come to the home show to see Bobbie, and he started a movie company just to make the movie about him. And Mr. Alexander, well, Bobbie made *him* famous. Everyone made a little something off that dog. It was all some sort of conspiracy to make money or get noticed," she said.

I didn't like that stupid woman with the bird on her head. I felt like biting her.

After the funeral was over, people gathered around Frank and Elizabeth to offer their condolences. I looked down into my father's grave at the small, wooden casket they had put him in. People were walking by and placing flowers on his grave. As I lay there, I glanced up at Frank and Elizabeth, and the photographer from the *Oregonian* snapped my picture.

I just wish Dad was closer to home.

I overheard Frank say to the reporter "I have lost one of the best friends a man could have. Bobbie loved me and I loved him. I have told my wife I would never have another pet. It is too much sorrow to lose them."

I don't think he meant that he was going to get rid of me, though.

Later, I followed Nova as she wandered around the grounds of the pet cemetery and past the rows of little white signs with each pet's name on them.

The cemetery was on a slope of ground behind the main building of the society. Tall cedars dotted the grounds, and at the bottom of the slope of ground was a small lake. Off in the distance, you could see Mount St. Helens and Mount Hood. I thought this was a nice place to be, and I was sure Dad would like it; but it was not Silverton. It was not home. He always told me that it was not just Frank, Elizabeth, Nova, or Leona that he was returning to. He wanted to come home to Silverton.

"Some places just get into your bones. And wherever you go, and however far you may travel, you always want to return to that place," he said to me.

This place on top of a hill overlooking the Columbia Slough in a city far removed from Silverton was not the place Dad would have chosen to be. But Frank and Elizabeth agreed with Colonel Hofer that the Humane Society would be a place where people could come to visit him. Leona, who was always a bit more cynical about people, thought that the folks in Portland wanted Dad for "political reasons." I don't know much about politics, I just wish Dad was closer to home.

Afterword

$\mathcal{B}$ OBBIE'S STORY REFUSES TO DIE WITH HIM. His legend lives on much like the old oak that once stood in town during Homer Davenport's day. Within a week after his funeral, he was front page news once again when Rin Tin Tin, the silent film star, came to the Oregon Humane Society and laid a wreath at Bobbie's grave. Photographers were on hand to capture his image.

For some time afterward, there were plans to erect a monument on the grounds of the Oregon Humane Society in Bobbie's memory. A small fund from donations was set up, and an artist was commissioned to design the memorial. However, not enough funds were ever accumulated to follow through on the project. The following article appeared at the time. The source is unknown. All errors in spelling and grammar are as they appear in the original.

NATION'S ANIMAL LOVERS PLAN
MEMORIAL SHAFT
FOR BOBBY OF SILVERTON

…To perpetuate the story of Bobby and his 3000 mile trek, the hardships he encountered, the hunger he endured-a story that has since been told the world over-the children of

Oregon and all dog lovers will be given an opportunity to sub-
scribe to the Bobby Memorial fund. A beautiful monument,
designed by an Oregon artist and dog-lover, Charlotte Mish,
will be erected in Portland's pet animal cemetery, the only
cemetery of its kind in the Northwest, situated in the
grounds of the Humane society's animal home, where Bobby of
Silverton is buried...Rin Tin Tin, famous motion picture dog
and his party have made the first contribution: $36 in all.
From this amount will be built the memorial. Bobbie remembered Oregon. Will you remember Bobbie?

❧

Interest in Bobbie may have waned, but it never completely disappeared. Over the years, the Brazier family continued to receive letters
from people who had read about him in various newspaper and magazine articles.

Over the decades that followed, Mrs. Brazier and her daughters,
Nova and Leona, and their daughters pasted the letters, news clippings, poetic tributes, and other mementos into numerous large scrapbooks that still exist today.

The following letter is typical of the many people who wrote to Bobbie when his story first came out. All the letters appear as the originals
including errors. It is reasonable that some significant letters were
passed around a great deal, and that some of them ended up missing.

Bloomington, Ill
May 14, 1924

Bobbie Brazier
The Collie Dog
Silverton, Ore:

Dear Bobbie:-
I suppose you will be surprised to get a letter. I am going to
tell you why I am writing to you, but first I'd better tell you
who I am. I am sure you are anxious to know.
*   I am a boy 12 years old and I live in Bloomington, and I go*
to school here too. I am in the 6th grade.

I love dogs more than anything else in the world. I have a little dog whose name is "Queen". She is a fox terrier. She is an awfully smart little dog.

I got a little bull dog for Christmas but she died about a month after I got her. I called her "Bubbles". I sure did cry too even if I am a boy.

But Bobbie I want to tell you what a smart doggie I think you are. I read the piece in the paper about you getting lost in Iowa and walking to Indiana then clear back to Oregon. Bobbie I just wish I could give you a great big hug. I think you are the most wonderfulst dog I ever heard to tell of to be so smart as to go all that way home alone. I bet you have a good home Bobbie or you'd never would have tried to walk all the way back and I bet the people who own you love you more than ever. I've never even seen you and I am sure I love you and I wish you were my dog. I'd be so good too you and I'd give you lots to eat and you could sleep in the house. But I'm sure Mr. and Mrs. Brazier love you too much to ever sell you to anybody for I know if you were my doggie I'd not sell you for all the money there was for I'd love you so much. We'd be great pals for I believe you would like me too. Do you think you would?

Bobbie I wonder if Mr. and Mrs. Brazier would send me a picture of you. It would make me so happy and you know I would keep it forever if they will. I'll send you a picture of my doggie and by return mail and you can look at it and say "that little boy wrote me a letter and he thinks I'm the nicest and smartest dog he every heard of" well, I hope your master will be so kind as to read this letter to you. If he will I just know you will understand it and Bobbie, please, won't you have them send me your picture and I will send you mine right away.

Good bye Bobbie, I wish I knew you.

Sincerely,
Howard Everingham
Bloomington, Illinois

Bobbie also received letters from some "non-human" fans:

March 28, 1924

Dear Collie: In our Dumb Animals magazine, which I take, I read how brave you were to find your way back to your master, all by yourself-that shows what a good, kind "master" you must have, for if he had treated you unkindly you never would have returned to him. Now about myself: I have a good home; I'm a black cat, weight about 20 pounds; have been written up a number of times in the papers. Inclosed is my last write-up. I go on board walk in harness, same as a dog. Have a crib to sleep in, same as babies have. Now, Collie, I hope you will let me hear from you, then I will tell you more about myself next time. If you have any pictures of yourself, I would like to have one. I have a library of over 20 books, all animal stories and I love to be read to. Be sure and answer your unknown friend.

"BLACKBERRY CHATFIELD"

Bobbie received many poetic tributes after his return and even after death. The following poem, by Peter Kellar of Portland, appeared on a flyer with a photo of Bobbie in front of his "castle." It was penned for his appearance at the Oregon State Fair in Salem that year.

'SILVERTON BOB'

You hunted garages and alleys,
Wended through by-ways and lanes;
Tramped over mountains and valleys,
Through sunshine, cold sleet and rains.
O'er pavement and rough road you traveled.
An automobile was your quest.
To find it along with your master
You headed home and the West.
Arriving here footsore and wearing
Tramping near three thousand miles.
Your master was tickled to see you
And greet you again with his smiles.

This week you have been highly honored
By City and County and State.
Thousands have come you to visit
And pat your wonderful pate.
Your Bungalow Home and Grand Collar
May you live to enjoy with the rest.
Of gifts that will come to you later
From friends you've made East and West.
And when your days here are ended
Your friends will attend that last job.
But this story will live with our children
We are proud of you "Silverton Bob."

⚓

While Bobbie and the Brazier family received letters, poems, and gifts
from all over the world—including England, Australia, and Germany—
the most significant letters were from the people who sheltered him on
his trip west. The exact route Bobbie took across seven states is not
known. However, it is through the following letters that both the family and the Oregon Humane Society were able to eventually determine
an approximate route.

Following is the letter from the woman at the summer cottage on the Tippecanoe River:

Mrs. William Dudley Pratt

March 24, 1924

Mr. G.F. Brazier: Silverton:

Dear Sir:
The enclosed picture appeared in an Indianapolis paper recently and I am wondering if I did not make the acquaintance of Bobbie last summer at my shack on the Tippecanoe River.

You say that the dog was lost in Wolcottville which is very far north in the State while the town of Wolcott is near and near the great State Road to Chicago.

I was sitting under a tree one summer day when I heard a splashing in the river and running up the hill came a Collie dog which I knew at once was seeking his master. He ran rapidly up the path past my cottage and out into the road which is a sort of private lane leading to but two place...

Much to our surprise, the dog came back several days later, very tired. We petted and fed him...We took care of him and wanted very much to keep him but we found him gone in the morning.

It was easy to see that he was distressed and in search of some one. I have been thinking that you might have lost him on the Monticello road which is the road leading from Chicago through northern Indiana...

Whether it was your Bobbie or not I am well pleased that you got your dog back. Nothing is more sorrowful than a dog longing for his master.

If you lose him again in Indiana I hope it will fall to my lot to find him.

I hope his toe-nails are growing again.

Very truly yours,
Sarah S. Pratt

This is a letter from Mr. Patton of Vinton, Iowa, one of Bobbie's detours:

Mar. 17, '24

Mr. G.F. Brazier,
Silverton, Ore.

Dear Sir,—some time last fall, a dog answering to the name of Bobby stopped at our car and we took him in the house, but he would not eat a bit until he had looked all over the house, upstairs and down and then he ate a good big meal and seemed quite contented all night. We gave him his breakfast in the morning and he stayed around just a little while and then left and that was the last we saw of him.

Did the horn of your car sound like a Dodge horn? We were stopped at the curb and just as we sound the horn to attract some one's attention, the dog ran up and jumped right into the car as though it were his own. Our girls owned a little dog named Bobby which had been run over and killed, so they tried that name on this dog and would liked to have kept it here, but it just stayed the one night and went on. It always seemed to be looking for some one. Please do not publish this letter for I am not looking for publicity. I just read in the Cedar Rapids Gazette of your dog traveling from Indiana to Oregon, and wonder if it could have possibly been the one that jumped into our car that night. Have you a Kodak picture of your Bobby, if so, I would like to received one just to see if it is the same dog.

Respectfully,
F.E. Patton

The Brazier family received this letter from Mrs. Plumb of Des Moines, Iowa:

July 3, 1925

My dear Mrs. Brazier,
I was greatly interested in an article appearing in the April number of Moral Welfare concerning the exploits of a collie "Bob" which you own. The picture so closely resembles a collie which we had the pleasure of entertaining for a few months during the summer and fall of 1923 that I am prompted to write you in the hope of establishing his identity.

I do not now recall whether it was July or August of 1923 the dog came to us wearing a heavy black strap collar with no name plate-license number or other mark of identification. He made his appearance during the night-and finding my nephew sleeping on the porch offered his paw to shake hands-after which he quietly went to sleep. In the morning after shaking hands with the family and receiving his breakfast he departed in the direction of the tourist camp which is only a few blocks from our house but in an hour or so came back to us and took up his abode. Although we were very fond of him-no effort was made to keep him.

Almost every day he made the trip in the direction of the tourist camp-which led us to believe he had been lost from there. We tried out different names, and found the name Bob seemed to suite him best.

While with us he disappeared for several days at one time and upon his return we found the heavy strap collar had been removed and a much lighter one substituted to which a fragment of rope was attached, showing plainly that someone had tried to keep him.

The latter part of November 1923-(the day after Thanksgiving to be exact) he again disappeared and has never returned to us.

It is unnecessary to say that we deeply regretted losing him, but have always hope he found his way back to his own people.

Am enclosing a couple of Kodaks showing the markings of the face but am sorry they do not show the entire body.

If the above data corresponds with what you already know

*of the dogs trip and you must have reason to believe that the
two Bobs are one and the same collie I would be glad to hear...*

The rest of the letter is missing and must have been lost in the shuffle back and forth between the interested parties.

⚜

The following letters are from Carrie Abbee from Denver, Colorado:

*G.F. Brazier
Silverton, Oregon*

*Dear Sir:-
The attached clipping in the Denver Post interested me owing
to the fact that late in November a large collie not very long
hair stopped at our house in fact ran up to our car as we were
driving into the garage and seemed very happy to see us. He
went into the house had his dinner and slept in the den in the
basement all night.*

*He was a very nice behaved dog and seemed very tired in
fact exhausted, was dusty and had burs in his hair.*

*We spoke of his being so tired and that he looked as though
he had a long hike, although he was in good condition. We
hope he would stay with us but in the morning he did not
even wait for his breakfast.*

*We lost our 14 year Collie in Sept of old age and would like
have had this one.*

*Would like awfully well to know if this was the same dog
and if you have a snap shot of him and would return it to you.*

*Yours truly
Carrie Abbee
Denver, Colo*

Mr. G.F. Brazier
Silverton, Oregon

Dear Sir:
Got Bob's picture and am delighted to tell you that with out
question of a doubt he was here and stayed all night at our
house on Dec. 6th. We had guests to dinner that night and we
made a lot over the dog and they too are certain he is the
same. Did not think from the picture in the paper he was the
same but his photo clears every doubt. He evidently returned
via the route the one you took, we are about 125 miles or a lit-
tle less south of Cheyenne.

The dog was very tired and we remarked several times that
he had no doubt, come a long distance. We thought he might
have followed a car in from the country.

I fixed his dinner and asked him to speak, which he did so
quickly and loud that it made me jump. We spoke of his
immense feet and what muscular hind legs he had and his
picture shows this.

We were in hopes the dog would have stayed but he left in
the morning. He minded every word which was some contrast
to our spoiled dog who never did a thing in his 14 years he did
not want to do.

We know it was Dec. 6th as we said it was three months
from the day our dog "Wonder" died and if he came to stay it
was a coinstance. (sic) He must have been shut up by some-
one when you lost him or he would have been found. If he
was it certainly caused him great hardship.

Yours sincerely,
Carrie Abbee

There were other people across the country who claimed they had seen
Bobbie on his trek west. Some came from other western states such as
Utah and California, but for one reason or another were not consid-
ered valid "sightings" by the family at the time. There were others who

aided Bobbie—such as the family in The Dalles, Oregon, and the people who gave him the ride to Denver—but their names remain unknown, as the documentation was lost. There were also accounts from garage owners and travelers in tourist camps in several states that report seeing Bobbie and feeding him before he was on his way.

For a number of years after Bobbie's death, his son Pal achieved a degree of celebrity as well. As the son of Bobbie, the Wonder Dog, he made appearances at fairs and other events. When his mate, Queenie, gave birth to a large litter of puppies, the newspapers carried this event as well. The pups were displayed at several pet and feed shops in Portland. The Brazier family had many offers from people wanting to own a grandchild of the famous Bobbie.

In 1932, at the height of the Depression, Silverton sponsored the first pet parade as a way to provide some inexpensive entertainment for the children of Silverton and to boost morale. It was also a way of remembering Bobbie. His son Pal was the first master of ceremonies. The parade is now an annual tradition and held the third Saturday in May, making it the longest tradition of its kind on the West Coast. The town comes alive with hundreds of local children—and their camera-toting parents—as they parade down Main Street on bicycles, wagons, scooters, and roller skates. Sometimes they have a favorite pet in tow, or sometimes they simply wear animal costumes. In the early years of the tradition, there were more farm animals such as horses, cows, pigs, chickens, rabbits, and geese. Today's animal spectrum includes dogs, cats, rabbits, snakes, rats, hamsters, ferrets, and pet birds to name a few. While many of the children do not know of Bobbie's story and the tradition behind the parade, they do know that it is about their pets and a chance to show them off, and about costumes and free candy and a chance to be silly. Some years' organizers find a Bobbie lookalike to ride in the parade to remind everyone how the whole thing got started.

Throughout the years, Mrs. Brazier was asked numerous times to retell the story of Bobbie. She continued to do radio and television programs even into the 1940s and 1950s. Both Leona and Nova were also contacted by writers, or just the plain curious, to recount their version of the story.

In later years, after the publication of the well known book *Lassie Come Home* in 1938, there were many who came to believe that this book was based on the exploits of Bobbie of Silverton. This is just one of the myths that have surrounded Bobbie. While the stories are alike in that they are both about collies who find their way home, that is where the similarity ends. Lassie was a fictional character based on Eric Knight's own dog, Toots, and set in England. While Mr. Knight may have heard of Bobbie's story, he also grew up in England with similar stories of collies finding their way home over long distances. Lassie has nothing on Bobbie, though. She only traveled a few hundred miles to return home.

After more than eighty years, there are a number of people determined to keep Bobbie's memory alive.

On a long wall on Water Street in Silverton, near the center of town, artist Lori Webb has painted a lively mural depicting Bobbie's story. Nearby, the Silverton Mural Society has erected a replica of Bobbie's famous castle and a life-sized, child-friendly sculpture of him as well. Both of these are within feet of the site of the Brazier's family restaurant.

Outside of Silverton, Bobbie's story is kept alive through the efforts of the Education Department of the Oregon Humane Society in Portland. Each year, busloads of school children tour the facility and the animal cemetery where Bobbie and his castle still reside.

The tour guide tells them of Bobbie's trek across seven states to return home to Silverton. As the facts sink in, each child struggles with thoughts of acceptance or disbelief. They contemplate the message of love and loyalty, and the importance of dogs having identification tags or microchips. Some of them may go home with a small amount of affection for a dog they never knew.

Why does Bobbie's story affect us so? Even those who refuse to believe it still try to imagine what would have motivated a dog to do such a thing. Was it instinct alone, or some reasoning ability?

Those who believe are unequivocally convinced of the truth of the story. They endow Bobbie with human-like qualities of love and loyalty. This, of course, is to the annoyance of those who do not believe, or who consider such anthropomorphism to be unreasonable and irrational.

Yet reason is thrown out the window when we relate to our dogs. Their wagging tails and soulful looks turn us into pudding. Surely, this is love. They stay by our side through thick and thin, through t-bone and hot dogs, through good moods and bad. Is this not loyalty? Some will say it is simply the dog bonding to his pack leader, and that the motivation is purely survival, not love. But any dog owner knows better.

The reason Bobbie's story has endured is that there are many who believe dogs are much more intelligent—and have much more genuinely emotional lives—than we give them credit for. They are capable of feelings that can only be put into the human words we call loyalty and love. There will be those who dispute this. However, those who believe in Bobbie and his story do not have to be convinced.

THE END

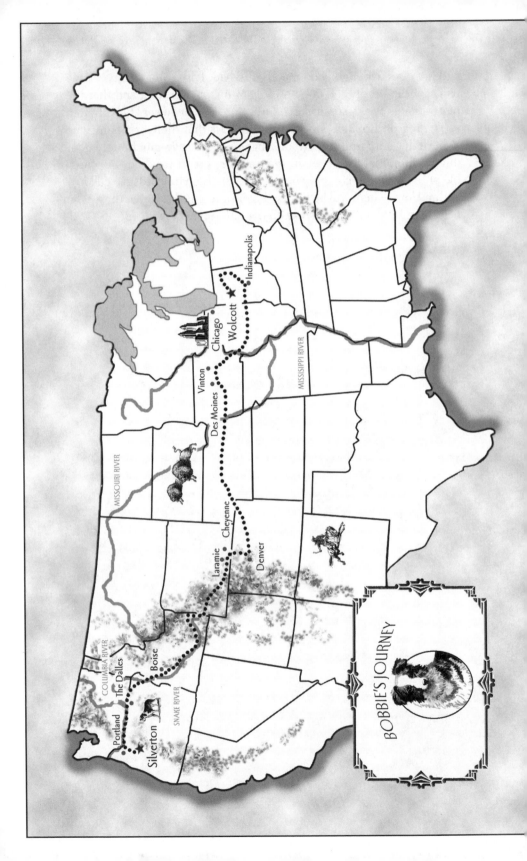

BOBBIE'S JOURNEY